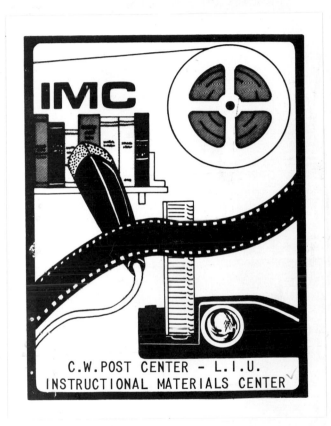

IMC

C.W. POST CENTER - L.I.U.
INSTRUCTIONAL MATERIALS CENTER

No Applause, Please

by Marilyn Singer

E. P. Dutton | New York

The publisher and the author gratefully acknowledge permission
to use the following material:
Page 38: "Résumé" from *The Portable Dorothy Parker*. Copyright
1926, 1954 by Dorothy Parker. Reprinted by permission of
The Viking Press.
Page 43: verse from "St. James' Infirmary" by Joe Primrose.
Copyright 1929 by Mills Music, Inc. Copyright renewed 1957.
All rights reserved. Used with permission.
Page 80: definition of "friend" from the *Random House Dictionary
of the English Language*. Copyright © 1966, 1973 by
Random House, Inc.

Library of Congress Cataloging in Publication Data

Singer, Marilyn   No Applause please.

SUMMARY: A fourteen-year-old poet-singer rethinks her career aspirations
and friendships when her stage-struck partner makes other plans.

[1. Friendship—Fiction. 2. Musicians—Fiction] I. Title.
PZ7.S6172No [Fic] 76-54274 ISBN 0-525-35975-3

Published simultaneously in Canada by Clarke,
Irwin & Company Limited, Toronto and Vancouver

Editor: Ann Durell
Printed in the U.S.A.   First Edition
10 9 8 7 6 5 4 3 2 1

To my parents,
and my Grandma Frieda

Part One

1

"Ruthie, why don't you sing that new song you made up?"

I should have expected it. When I was younger, I was always performing at family dinners—usually without any prompting. I'd sing, dance, act, spell hard words, and discuss what I considered philosophical issues such as cheating at school and what I would do with one million dollars. No wonder my quiet cousin Carole, whom I haven't seen for five years, couldn't stand me. But that was when I was younger. Now that I'm fourteen I have no desire to perform for my Uncle Sol and my Aunt Claire, who were at that moment dozing respectively in my favorite armchair and on the sofa, or my cousin Bernard, who was reading the stock market reports, or his wife Gail or anyone else—almost—except on the stage, which

is why my friend Laurie and I are writing songs. However, my mother hasn't gotten the message.

"I'd rather not," I said.

"Oh, go ahead. It's a nice song," she said.

"It's not finished yet."

"Sing what's finished, then."

Cousin Gail interrupted, "That's okay, Pearl. I know
how an artist hates to present something incomplete."
She winked at me conspiratorially.

I flashed an insincere smile. Artist my ass! Gail always
prides herself on her child psychology.

"Come on, Pearl. I'll help you with the dishes." She
winked at me again.

"So, Gail, when you going have baby?" my grandma
cut in.

"Leave her alone, she's got time," Mom said quickly.

My dad, playing solitaire at the dining room table,
snorted, and Mom gave him a look.

Then she and Grandma and Gail started clearing plates
and brushing crumbs and washing pots and pans. I decided it was a good time to escape. I wanted to get over
to Laurie's so we could continue The Dream. I had some
great new ideas. . . .

"Ruthie, what do you think you're doing? Aren't you
going to help us?" Mom yelled just as I reached the door.

"Okay," I answered and slumped into the kitchen, trying to avoid looking at the forlorn carcass of the turkey
we'd just feasted on. I hate turkey; it always looks like it
could leap up, headless, and start wobbling around any
minute. In fact, I hate meat, but every time I tell my
mother, she asks me what kind of kook I'm turning out to
be. Anyway, I headed straight for the sink, but wouldn't
you know it—

"Ruthie, wrap the turkey and put it in the refrigerator,"
Mom said.

"I'm wiping the dishes," I said, quickly grabbing a wet pot.

She had seen me dash for it, though, and she shook her head. "Sometimes I wonder about you, Ruthie."

"Sometimes I do too, Mom."

"So, Gail," she said, immediately forgetting what we'd just been talking about the way she always does, "how's your new house?"

"Oh, it's fantastic," Gail began.

I hate the way *fan* comes out of her nose instead of her mouth, but I realize that's prejudiced. Still, couldn't she have taken speech in college?

"Two bedrooms. One has a big, bay window. . . ."

Hope you have big, bay curtains, I said to myself, stifling a giggle. Oh my God, I've really got to get over to Laurie's before I make a fool of myself, I thought.

"Rootie," shouted Grandma—well, it wasn't exactly a shout; it's just that my grandma speaks very loudly on account of everybody assuming she's deaf, which she isn't, and speaking loudly to her. Anyway, Grandma yelled, "Rootie, how come you din eat much tonight? Din you like my food?"

Now there would have been no point telling her I don't like turkey, which she didn't make, or that I wasn't hungry, so I said, "You know I love your cooking. Didn't you see me stuffing it in, Grandma? All that stuffed cabbage and challah."

"You din eat toikey."

"Sure I did, Grandma." It was true—she didn't have to know I'd only taken one piece.

"You sick?"

"No, Gram, I'm fine." But I won't be much longer if I don't get out of here, I added silently.

"The bathroom has blue tiles and a sunken tub," Gail was still talking.

"That sounds wonderful," Mom exclaimed. I knew that evening after everyone left she'd say, "Sunken bathtubs yet, and look at the cheap wine they brought for dinner."

"And the garden. . . ."

Oh help, I thought, and then I must have set the world's record for drying dishes.

"Ma, I'm finished. I'm going over to Laurie's," I said, halfway out the door.

"Ruthie, we have company," she hollered.

How well I know, I thought. "I'll be back later," I yelled and ran across the street as fast as I could.

2

"Did you get rid of your relatives?" Laurie grinned when she answered the door.

"No, they got rid of me. It was Ruthie-sing-us-a-song time again."

"Speaking of which, we ought to rehearse."

Laurie and I are going to sing in the school show. I am very nervous about it, having written the songs. I am also nervous because, as I said before, I really haven't performed since I was a kid—and even then I couldn't take it being, well, *formal.* I remember when I was really little —around three, I think—and we went to a summer resort in the Catskills. Everyday I went into the dark, musty auditorium and climbed onto the stage. Behind the curtain were cases of seltzer and chocolate syrup. I never knew why or how they always managed to disappear for the evening shows featuring singers, impersonators, and cartoons. I was scared of the cartoons; I think I couldn't stand cats being blown up and dogs bopped on the heads and some villain or another being shot in the pants. Anyway, I'd step out on the dark stage and sing into a dead mike. The only people who saw me were the handyman and my parents. How was I to know the handyman had a big mouth?

One Saturday night, we assembled for the dreaded cartoons. Rick Bissell (Mom says that was his name), smiling M.C., stepped out.

"Tonight." Grin. Grin. "We have a special surprise for you all." Teeth. Teeth. "We have in our audience a little miss who can sing up a storm." I sat there wondering who was going to make a fool of herself. "Please give a big hand to our own Ruthie Zeiler." Loud applause. I didn't move.

"Go on, Ruthie, it's you," Mom nudged.

"Get up there, honey." Dad smiled.

I looked at both of them. They knew all along I was going to be "introduced." I would have yelled "traitors" at them, but I didn't know the word. So instead, I shouted, "No," burst into tears, and ran out of the hall. So much for my singing career. As I said, I performed all the time for relatives, maybe even strangers. But that was offstage. Then I stopped. I think I decided it made people think I was precocious. Now I only sing for Laurie—but that's about to change. Once again, I'm going public. And I'm scared.

Laurie isn't scared at all. She is a terrific strong soprano (I am an alto—or maybe a tenor), and she sings all the time, anywhere, at a moment's notice. Funny, nobody has ever called her precocious. Of course, I haven't told her how good her voice is; I figure she's conceited enough about her voice, with all the compliments she always gets. I just say we sound good together. Laurie also plays guitar well —something I just can't seem to do. But she can't write songs at all, so I guess we make a good team.

"Yeah, we'll rehearse—but let's continue The Dream first."

"No, we'll rehearse first. Work before pleasure." Laurie often speaks in clichés. And besides, rehearsing is pure pleasure for her. "Have you figured out what you're going to wear yet?"

Now if there's one thing I don't think about, it's clothes. I gave Laurie one of my disapproving glances. "I am not a fashion show."

"I know, stupid, but we still have to look good. My mom says I can wear some of her eye shadow and liner."

"You planning on wowing the boys in the front row?" I was being nasty, but I couldn't help it. My songs are about being yourself, being natural, and here was Laurie talking about makeup and stuff.

"There might be an agent in the audience," she said haughtily.

"Sure, just dying to take two fourteen-year-olds under his wing and book them into the hottest clubs in town. Is this another one of Sylvia's bright ideas?"

Sylvia is Laurie's mother. I have called her Sylvia since I was five because she asked me to. She is always pushing show biz at Laurie.

Laurie ignored my remark about her mother and said, "Who said anything about *two* fourteen-year-olds?"

That did it. I wasn't in such a hot mood to start with— what with my relatives and all. And now Laurie was being rotten. I felt tears forming, but I didn't want Laurie to see how much she'd hurt me. So I said in a calm voice,

"If that's the case, you don't need me to rehearse. See you some time." And I dashed out of the house.

I couldn't go home and face the relatives again, so I headed for a little playground I always go to when I want to be alone. It has a slide, a sandbox, a basketball court which gets all icy in the winter, and a couple of swings shaped like horses. A few little kids were playing in the sand when I got there. I went and sat on one of the horses; if I looked funny, I didn't care. I used to sit on the horses all the time when I was little and pretend I was a knight riding to save a lady in distress. I never pretended I was the lady because her part was so boring. I sat still and tried not to cry, but it didn't work. I bawled like a baby. Fortunately, the little kids ignored me. Finally, I wiped my eyes and decided to go home.

I am not going to make up first with Laurie this time. I am always the one to make up—even if I haven't started the fight. Laurie can just need me first this time. And The Dream can wait.

3

I like school—unlike a lot of kids I know. I really like
learning stuff. Mom says I always was curious—that's
probably why I walked and talked at such an early age.
My father has a different explanation; he says I was vac-
cinated with a phonograph needle. That's an old joke and
it's supposed to be funny. I also like school because it
gets me out of my house. Mom spends all day reading
things like *Reader's Digest,* when she isn't doing housework. Then, she and Dad spend all evening watching
T.V. I think that's so boring. But what is most boring is
they'd just love it if I stayed home and watched T.V. with
them. I told them I have plenty of time to be senile, but
that didn't go over too well.

The only thing I don't like about school are the other

kids. For one thing, all the kids in my class are older than me because I skipped a grade. They're always fussing about clothes and boys, or clothes and girls, or clothes and rock. I don't have anything against rock, but personally, I'd rather listen to Tchaikovsky. *They* don't even know who he is. I guess that's why I'm friends with Laurie, whom I haven't spoken to this week on account of our fight. Not that she listens to Tchaikovsky either, but at least she doesn't think it funny that I do—or that I write poetry. We both like animals and dancing and food. She can make *real* french fries. We fight a lot, but we always make up—at least we did in the past. I think people who never fight aren't really close friends.

Today at school everyone was talking about Shelley Sugarman's party to which I haven't been invited. I felt pretty bad about it—not that I really wanted to go that much—but the only other person who wasn't invited was Maureen McTeagle, who wears white socks and dribbles when she talks. I don't see any resemblance between us.

Shelley is an actress—is, not wants to be. She does summer stock somewhere in Cape Cod. She also thinks she's God's greatest gift. Somehow, nobody seems put off by this because Shelley is undoubtedly the most popular girl in our class—maybe even in school. Her party is going to be a costume affair with everyone dressing as The Me Nobody Knows. I overheard Shelley telling a friend that she thought up that idea because it's a psychological theater game she's played in acting class. I wasn't impressed.

When lunchtime came, I raced to the cafeteria. I wanted to get there before the crowds so I could get a seat by myself. I also wanted to give Laurie an opportunity to sit with me. For the past few days, I've seen her join a group of cheerleaders and jocks at the far side of the room. I couldn't believe my eyes. I mean I know Laurie can be silly, but I never thought she'd be this silly. I figure she must be doing it to annoy me. Just as I got my seat, she came in with the sports set and went to their table without a glance at me. I felt like I was going to cry again and that would've been really embarrassing, so I pulled out some paper and started writing instead. I write best when I'm depressed. But I didn't get too far along because Shelley swept into sight, her followers tagging along.

"Looks like we'll have to sit here," she said gaily, ignoring me.

And they all sat down.

"Catastrophic news, children. Peter is not coming to el fete," she said tragically. Shelley thinks it cute to mix up Spanish and French. What is so cute about it I can't tell you.

"Why not?" said her friend Roz.

"He's off to the Cape to see about the renovations of the theater."

Peter is the director of the company, and if that little fifteen-year-old twirp thought this guy in his thirties was coming to her dumb-ass party, she must be gaga.

"What are you going to change your name to, Shel?" Mitch changed the topic. He was one of the honored, which meant that Shelley liked him, which meant that he could call her Shel.

"How about Shelley Sugar?" Roz said.

Shelley glared at her over the bridge of her plastic-surgeried nose.

"I'm only kidding," Roz retorted defensively.

"How about Shelley Sinclair?" Luanne suggested.

"Too WASP."

"Pardon me," sniffed 100 percent WASP Luanne.

All this time, I kept my head buried in my paper, but I was listening, not writing.

"Actually, I'm thinking of using my middle name and

calling myself Shelley Saper, which sounds better than Sugarman."

"Saper! How'd you get a name like that for a middle name?"

"It's my mother's maiden name."

"You're lucky you've got a useful middle name. I hate mine," Mitch said.

"What is it?"

"Oh no."

"Come on, Mitch."

"Yeah, what is it?"

"All right, it's Marcus."

Giggles and rib-poking and a mad search for who had the weirdest name there. Then, I swear I don't know what made me do it, but I found myself saying, "I don't think any of you have a name as strange as I do."

They turned with one head and stared as if my lunch had spoken instead of me. And they all waited for Shelley to say the first words.

"Ru–thie," she separated the syllables. "What's so strange about that?"

Everyone giggled. I kept cool.

"Nothing. It's my middle names that are unusual."

"Really? What are they?"

I took a sip of juice. "Robertinalina Nightingale."

After a pause, everyone cracked up.

"Oh my God."

"That's a good one."

"Tell us another."

"Did you just make it up?"

"Oh brother."

I was the only one who wasn't laughing.

"Excuse me," I said, getting up.

"Wait," Shelley said, tears and makeup running down her face. "How did you think that up?"

"I didn't." I was perfectly deadpan. "My grandfathers were both named Robert. One grandmother was Tina, the other Lina. My parents put all the names together in honor of them."

Everyone stopped laughing.

"Are they all—uh—passed away?" Roz asked.

"Yes."

They looked ashamed—except for Shelley. "And what about Nightingale?" she asked.

"I made that up," I smiled.

Just then the bell rang for our next class. As I pushed into the hall, I felt a tap on my shoulder. It was Shelley.

"Kid, you're a good actress. How'd you like to come to my party?"

"You having a party?" I said, playing dumb.

"Tomorrow night," she played right along.

"All right—unless I've planned something I forgot about."

"Great. Oh, and it's a costume affair. The Me Nobody Knows. Why don't you come as Robertinalina Nightingale?"

I tried to be suave. "I might," I said.

4

My first thought was to run and tell Laurie I'd been invited to Shelley's party. Laurie is a grade below me and Shelley doesn't know her, but she knows Shelley—like everybody else in school. Anyway, I wanted to tell her, but then I remembered that we weren't speaking. I didn't intend to go to the party. That would be the really cool move, I thought. To be invited to a Shelley Sugarman extravaganza and not show up. But then I got to thinking that if I don't tell Laurie I've been invited, and if I don't show up, she'll simply think I wasn't invited. If I do go, when we finally get to speaking again, I can casually drop some of the things that happened there into the conversation. Or if I don't go, I could super-casually say I was invited, but didn't go. Which is more effective? Of course,

I am not taking into consideration whether or not I *want* to go. Hell, I'll decide tomorrow.

Dinner tonight was very slow. My mom and grandma, as usual, were bustling about with plates of food while my dad sat there, Sultan-like in his special chair that nobody else is allowed to sit on—at least during meals or when he plays solitaire. But when everyone finally sat down, the meal seemed to stretch into eternity. No one had anything to say. Finally, my mom spoke. It seemed like she was dragging out the words, one by one.

"So, what happened at school today, Ruthie?"

"Nothing much. I got invited to Shelley Sugarman's party."

"The child actress?" Now why did she have to add "child"?

"She performs in summer stock."

"Such a profession for a young girl. What kind of childhood could she have? Surrounded by all those actors. Everybody knows what *they're* like." My mother was off again, talking to no one in particular.

"I hope you're not going," my dad said warningly.

"I haven't decided yet. And anyway, it's for my class and not for actors."

"I wonder what kind of parents that girl has. They must not care very much." Mom was still at it. But since no one cared to argue with her, she quieted down.

"Rootie, I din see Laurie this week." That was my grandma. She likes Laurie a lot because—and this is one of Laurie's best traits—she talks to Gram like a human being.

How could I answer? I didn't want to say we'd had a fight because my mom would start in again: "That Laurie is so conceited. Can't you see she's using you?" Etcetera. But I hate lying—especially to Gram.

"Uh . . . Laurie's pretty busy."

"Oh," my mom was quick to pounce. "And what's she so busy about? Studying for a change?"

"She's trying out for the cheerleading squad."

"In the spring?" My dad arched his brows.

"Yes, for next year." For all I knew, it might have been true.

"I guess you won't be seeing her so much, if she makes it. Maybe you'll spend more time with us, then," Mom said.

Then I felt it. That familiar lump—like congealed cereal in my stomach. It would work its way into my chest, up into my throat until I'd have to let it out by yelling or crying. This time I'd stop it before the rest happened.

"If you'll excuse me, I have a lot of homework to do."

"What about the dishes?"

"Let her do work. I do dishes," Grandma said. I wanted to hug her, but I didn't. I dashed to my room. Just in time too, because I ended up crying anyway.

Tonight, Grandma came into my room. I was reading Emily Dickinson's poetry. Whenever I'm upset, I read Emily. She calms me down.

"You going to bed, Rootie?"

"Yes, Gram."

"Listen, how about I should tell you story?" My grandmother came here from Rumania when she was fourteen. She can't read or write, but she can tell the most fantastic stories. I hope I never get too old for them.

"Yes, please." I was excited. She hadn't told me a story in a while. "How about the one where the lord is mean to his lady and she chops down the tree to show him it's hollow, like his heart?" I loved that one.

"No, this new one. Once upon time, there was two sisters, both princesses, Zoika and Irinuca. They very close, but they fight all time. Over silly things. 'My hair is prettier yellow,' Zoika say even though both have same hair. 'I sing better,' Irinuca say, even though both have beautiful voices. One day, they have really bad fight. And is so silly, they soon forget what it is about. But still they don't speak. Finally, they are both married with babies. Zoika decide to visit Irinuca and bring her baby present. That will make them friends again. And she bring her child for Irinuca to see.

"Irinuca is lying in great bed with satin covers and lace gown. Her baby is wearing pink robe and white bonnet. 'Well, my sister. It been years. What do you say?'

"Zoika answer, 'I bring present and my baby, Catinca, for you to see.'

" 'Thank you. Here is my baby, Maria. Beautiful, yes?'

" 'Yes, but mine is prettier.'

"And so they start to fight all over again. This time, years and years go by. Zoika is dying. This time, Irinuca decide to end fight. She bring dress for Zoika. When she arrive, doctor is just pronouncing Zoika dead.

" 'Oh, and I never had chance to forgive her,' say Irinuca, 'Well, here is dress I bring. She will be buried in it.'

"At that, Zoika open her eyes and say, in weak voice, 'Oh no. The one I make is prettier.'

"And they fight again so much that Irinuca's head boist and she and Zoika die together and are both buried in dresses they make."

When Grandma finished, I cracked up. First, I laughed and laughed. Then, I started to cry, with laughter in between.

"You like it?" Gram asked.

"Oh, Gram." I was choking by then, so I just hugged her. When I calmed down, she tucked me in, just the way she did when I was little.

"You sleep now."

"I will . . . thank you, Grandma."

She turned to leave.

"Gram," I called after her.

"What, my little Rootie?" Gram is the only one I let call me "little."

"I'll make up with Laurie tomorrow."

She turned slowly. "Din know you fight." Then, she winked and left my room.

I guess I am a jellyfish, but I'd rather be that than a mule.

5

It was Shavuos today, so I was home from school. I have no idea what Shavuos means and neither do my parents, but it's a Jewish holiday and all the other Jewish kids were staying home. They probably don't know what it's about either, but a holiday is a holiday. Laurie was also home and I figured I'd go over and see her. I knew it was going to be hard, so I dawdled over breakfast.

"Will you come shopping with me?" Mom asked.

"Can't," I mumbled. "Going to see Laurie."

"I thought she was busy."

"Not today." I made a quick exit and a slow walk. But I got to her door just the same. Okay, kid, now, I told myself and rang the bell. Laurie's bratty brother, Stuie, answered.

"What do you want?" He had maple syrup all over his face.

"Stuart, you know perfectly well what I want," I said in my best mother voice.

"She's still sleeping."

"No, I'm not, Stuie, and get away from that door." Laurie's face took a turn for the worse when she saw me. "Oh, I thought it was Carole."

"Carole who?" I demanded. This was worse than I thought it would be.

"Carole Schneider." Carole Schneider is cheerleading captain, as bouncy as they come. I'm positive she even bounces in her sleep, like a big, rubber ball.

"What's she coming over for?"

"If you must know, it's to teach me a few cheers."

"Oh . . . well, I thought I'd tell you not to call me tonight because I'm going to Shelley Sugarman's party."

"I thought you couldn't stand her. And besides, I wasn't going to call you."

I felt really deflated, so I did the only thing I could—I forced Laurie to be honest. "Why not?" I said bravely.

"Because . . . because. Oh for God's sakes, because I'm *angry* at you, you snotty little creep."

We stared at each other with tight faces.

"Look at who's talking. Miss Boom-Boom of Walker High."

Then, all of a sudden, we began to laugh. My last remark was so absurd, we just couldn't help it. And while we were wiping our eyes, I said, "Come on, let's rehearse."

"Can I watch?" Stuie had wandered in.

"You can watch that hole in the wall and see if a mouse crawls out of it," Laurie retorted.

"Okay," Stuie chirped and we cracked up again.

Rehearsal went really well. We sang terrifically.

"Are you really going to Shelley's party?" Laurie asked when we took a break.

"Oh, I thought it might be interesting material for a novel."

"Ha."

"No, really."

Laurie frowned.

"What's up?"

"That leaves me with nothing to do."

"How about Carole Schneider?" I had to dig that in.

"Oh, she's fine for a couple of hours, but who'd want to spend an evening with her?"

"I don't know, maybe she's the perfect date," I wise-cracked.

"Yeah, never a hair out of place . . . she goes out with college guys."

"Maybe she puts out." That disgusting expression I reserve for my nastiest moments.

"Who? Carole? Never. Don't touch me, don't touch! I'm a virgin."

"I'm a 'vergin,' " I said, hillbilly style. It was dumb, but we laughed.

"What do you think sex is like?"

"The man puts his penis . . ."

"No, idiot. I said what do you *think* it's like, not what *is* it?"

"I dunno, but I hope it's fun."

"Of course it's fun; people have been doing it for years."

"They've also been getting lung cancer for years. Let's rehearse some more."

"No, let's continue The Dream."

I've promised to describe The Dream, so here goes. In The Dream, whichever one it happens to be, our fantasies of the moment are enacted. At present, Laurie is becoming a famous film star—of the thirties. I am her manager, her leading man, her rival, and any other parts that come up. Just then, I was her best friend.

"M.G.M. has offered me a bit part in their latest picture . . . I play a prostitute."

"Honestly, Laurie," I yelled, out of character. I hate it when she does something vulgar like that—it ruins all the romance of the fantasy. She thinks it's very grown-up and authentic. Sometimes I think she's never heard of women's liberation. She ignored me and went on.

"I don't have to take off my clothes, and I get to kiss Clark Gable."

Laurie and I watched *Mutiny on the Bounty* two weeks ago. We love old movies.

"Big deal," I muttered. *I* do not have a crush on Clark Gable. He's too smooth and handsome for me. I happen to like Franchot Tone much more. But Laurie adores Clark.

"Come on, Ruthie, unfair."

"Why don't you take the bit part of his girl friend instead, Constance?" I was back in my role. "Can't have you typed as the Bad Girl."

"Hmmm, I think you may be right. I'll speak to my manager. . . . Hello, Bennett."

I lowered my voice, "Hello, Constance, taking the M.G.M. part?"

"*Not* the prostitute, I want the girl-friend role."

"Lulu Marsh has that." Lulu was the dreaded rival.

"You can fix that, Bennett, dear."

"You can fix it better than I can. Just trot down to the studio, read both parts, and do the best job for the girl friend."

"Oh, Bennett, you're the best in the biz."

Oh, brother, I thought. She was getting all cooey and trite again. I hoped she'd improve. "Ms. Garnett, we'd like you to perform this scene with Mr. Gable." I don't think that's how screen tests work, but it was more fun. "Your lines are 'Oh, Paul, Paul,' and then you fling yourself in his arms and sob."

Laurie did a Greta Garbo and threw herself at me, nearly knocking me over. While she was sobbing in my arms, Stuie walked in. We both jumped up at once, horribly embarrassed.

"Which one's the boy?" he snickered.

"Shut up, you idiot, can't you see your sister's upset?" I hoped Laurie would take the hint, which she did, and started to shake as if she were crying.

"What's the matter?"

"She lost out on cheerleading." That wasn't too bright of me, and Laurie gave me an ugly look. "Now, scram!"

Stuie left.

"What did you do that for?" she asked.

"Sorry, it just slipped out. I don't like your baby brother thinking we're queer or something."

"Oh, he won't because we're not."

"True." But I was—am—a little worried. Not worried that we're lesbians or anything. I mean, we never kiss, and I'm certainly not attracted to Laurie or her to me. But we spend a lot of time wrapped up in our fantasies. I mean, if other people knew, they'd certainly think we're weird. Sometimes, I want to stop The Dream completely, but I always get lured back. I guess because it's always so much better than what is really happening.

"Let's continue," Laurie said. "The good part's coming up."

"No. Sorry, Laur, but Stuie blew it."

"Okay," she said grumpily.

"We'd better rehearse some more anyway. Then I've got to get ready for Shelley's party."

"You're really going?"

"Yup." I've decided it is good to see more of the world.

6

Blue jeans and a loose Indian blouse and a pad of paper tucked under my arm. That was my costume for Shelley's party. I decided that The Me Nobody Knows is Me, period—and also the fact that I'm an aspiring poet ("poetess," Mom would say, a totally unnecessary distinction). Maybe I was being a little too subtle, or maybe too obvious, but too bad, I *was* being honest.

Dad protested against driving me to the party and picking me up, so I told him if he'd take me there, I'd get someone to take me home. At that suggestion he protested even more vehemently ("vehemently" is a great word; I just learned it recently and now it seems to be popping up everywhere). "I'm not going to let any fourteen-year-old who probably drives without a license take my daughter home."

24

"No, Dad, I meant I'd get another parent to do it."

He grumbled some more. "Eleven sharp, then."

"You mean you'll pick me up?"

"Eleven sharp." And he went back to his newspaper.

My father has to protest everything before he finally agrees to do it—and he almost always agrees eventually. It makes things confusing unless you understand his style.

It wasn't until I slid into the car that I realized how nervous I was. I mean, I knew mostly everyone who was going to be there, but only because we are in the same class. I don't really know them, and they certainly don't know me. For the first time that day I wished Laurie were with me. Oh well, I tried to comfort myself, if it's really bad I can sit in the toilet for a while or even leave, except then I'd have to call Mom and Dad and explain and that'd be a drag. The toilet was a better idea. Or the backyard. Surely Shelley had a backyard. After all, even we did.

"Eleven sharp," Dad warned once again as I stepped out of the car.

"Don't worry," I said.

"And don't drink anything."

"What if I'm thirsty?" I was being snide.

"You know what I mean, smarty-pants. . . . Have a good time," he added gruffly.

"Thanks, Dad."

I felt a surge of panic and was ready to rush after the retreating car, when the door opened. A short, plump woman peered out. "I thought I heard a car," she smiled at me, "Come on in. I'm Shelley's mother."

I walked in, listening for party noises. There weren't any. "I'm Ruth Zeiler, eh, Ms. Sugarman."

"Sally."

"I beg your pardon?"

"My name's Sally."

I knew right then I couldn't bring myself to call her Sally. But I nodded and smiled.

"You're a bit early."

"Shelley said eight o'clock."

"Oh, that always means eight-thirty."

"Where is she?"

"Still getting ready. . . . Have a seat."

So, I was the first one there. I felt my face getting hot. What was I going to say to this woman?

"What are you dressed as?" she asked politely. "Such a clever idea Shelley had, don't you think?"

"Yes, very clever. You must be very proud of her," I avoided her question. I figured I'd have to explain myself enough that night—unless I managed to hide.

"Oh, Shelley is a good girl. Very talented, very bright. . . . But sometimes she's a bit of a snob—a little pretentious, if you know what I mean."

I didn't know what to say. It seemed weird that Shelley's own mother was criticizing her daughter to someone she'd just met.

"Oh, really," I answered. Boy, how dumb.

"Wait till you see her costume. . . . You'll see what I mean. Quite unlike yours. I can tell you're a straightforward person."

I don't blush, but if I did, I sure would've. Instead, I coughed and changed the subject, or so I thought. "I'd like to see her act."

"Haven't you? She's always acting."

Fortunately, I didn't have to reply because Shelley herself flounced into the room in a safari outfit, khaki shorts and jacket, helmet, binoculars, and knapsack. I never thought anyone could look sexy in khaki, but Shelley did. The fact that she was wearing a halter top under the open jacket and already has a big bust probably helped.

"Why, Ruthie, you made it. I'm *so* glad," she emoted. "Has mother been entertaining? She had aspirations of becoming an actress, you know."

Ms. Sugarman's—Sally's—nostrils flared slightly and her smile looked pinched, but she said, "Actually, Ruth has been entertaining me. . . . Now, be a good hostess, dear, and take her to the garden."

As Shelley led me to the backyard, I asked her what she was supposed to be.

"Ah, The Me Nobody Knows is an adventurer, a seeker after the truth. Hence, the safari outfit," she added, in case I missed its significance.

"Clever," I said. Your mother is right, I thought.

The garden was decorated with candles. No colored light bulbs here. Just candles and the flowers that were doing their spring blooming. It was really lovely. A table was set discreetly to one side, bearing a huge bowl of what I guessed was punch and platters of little thingies. Sandwiches, I wondered.

"What is The You Nobody Knows?" Shelley asked.

Just as I was about to answer, the bell rang distantly.

"Excuse me," she said and swished into the house.

The yard began to fill up pretty quickly after that. And, boy, the costumes. Roz was all in fluffy pink and giggling a lot. Mitch had on a beret and Toulouse-Lautrec beard. There were slinky ladies and weight-lifting guys, revolutionaries, royalty, and other types. I think they thought it was a Come-as-I-Wish-I-Were party rather than The Me Nobody Knows. I decided to sit under a lilac bush, smell the flowers, and observe the scene.

Shelley would take each new arrival by the arm and lead her or him to what she must've thought was an appropriate group. The bunch nearest me was having a lot of trouble making polite conversation, and I wondered if they represented what was going on all over the yard. But I reckoned it wasn't because what they call Gay Laughter rang out from several places and, besides, most of the people knew each other from school. Every so often, Shelley's voice would pierce through the buzz with comments like, "You're too much" and "Splendido." Frank Maginetto thumped by, with his girl, Susie Something-or other. He is the class hood and was wearing, of course, a muscle shirt. I couldn't understand why he'd been invited until I overheard Shelley telling Roz what a "fascinating sociological study he is."

"I thought there was going to be booze," Frank grunted.

"The punch is good," Susie stuttered. Fourteen and already she was well on her way to being a doormat.

"All fruit and no boot," Frank snarled. Then he cocked his head and a smile dragged itself across his face. "Hey, that was pretty good . . . I rhymed."

"It was *wonderful*, Frank," Susie fluttered. I swear to God she said "wonderful." Can you believe it?

Then, they walked away. I think they crawled into the bushes somewhere to neck, but I couldn't be sure. I sat and waited for the next people to pass. While I was waiting, I got an idea for a poem. Well, not a poem really, just a silly verse, a commentary. The first line just came to me:

The Sugar Woman's search for truth.

I liked it because of the play on "Sugarman." The second line was a natural:

Wouldn't fool a Baby Ruth.

I loved it. I potzed around a little and then the last lines flashed:

'Cause what she thinks is her creation
Is sweetly sickening imitation.

I giggled to myself when I finished it. I thought "sweetly sickening," rather than "sickeningly sweet" was pretty sophisticated stuff. I was so busy smothering my giggles I didn't notice this guy standing over me until he said, "What's so funny?" I must've jumped fifty feet.

"Don't do that!" I yelled when I hit the ground.

"Well, what is so funny?" He sat down next to me. That's when I got a good look at him. He looked about eighteen. He had dark, curly hair, huge brown eyes, and a big nose. I like big noses. They have character, Mom says, and I agree. I thought he was awfully good-looking —and there was also something familiar about him.

"It's just a poem I was writing."

"Can I see?"

I hesitated. Suppose he was a good friend of Shelley's? Suppose he figured out what my poem meant and told her? Then I thought, so what? Shelley may have invited me to this boring party, but she still didn't like me and neither did her friends. "Okay," I said and showed him the paper.

"Did you really write this?" he said when he finished laughing.

"I told you I did," I said crossly.

"I've got to have a copy . . . er . . . Ruth."

"How did you know my name is Ruth?"

"Says so in the poem, doesn't it?"

I felt my face get hot, so I acted angry, "Well, yeah, in fact, it does."

"It's very clever."

"Listen," I demanded. "Who are you anyway?"

"I'm Jason."

"Jason who?" As if his last name mattered!

He smiled mischievously, "Jason Sugarman."

My stomach dropped into my shoes. "You're . . . Shelley's brother," I choked.

"Yep."

"Oh God," I leaped up, but Jason grabbed my arm.

"Hold it, it's all right. What you wrote is true."

I didn't say anything.

"You're a very perceptive young woman," he said solemnly.

I stared at him.

"Now sit down and relax. Want to smoke some dope?"

I sat down obediently. Jason lit a joint and offered it to me. "No, thanks," I managed to croak.

"It's good stuff."

"No."

"Okay." He was quiet through the whole joint and so was I. Then, he spoke, "Shelley Sugarman is an extremely spoiled youngster whose parents give her everything she wants—particularly her father. Her life is spent manipulating people in search of the one figure who can manipulate her. Since her brother, Jason, is the only person as adept at manipulation as Shelley, it follows that Shelley is constantly in search of the equivalent of Jason." He stopped.

"How did you figure out all that?" I asked, kind of scared by his language and the weird, robot-way he spoke.

"From my psychiatrist." Then he grinned, looking more normal again.

I was about to ask him what he planned to do about all this manipulation business, which I didn't understand that well anyway, when Shelley called out, "All right, guests. It's time for The Truth Game in which everyone reveals The Me Nobody Knows. I'll begin. Shelley Sugarman, age fifteen, adventurer and truth-seeker. My journeys take me far into my being and out into the world."

I wanted to puke. At that moment, I was really glad I wrote the poem. When she finished, a few people clapped.

She stopped them. "No applause, please. I'm merely revealing myself. Now, Roz. . . ."

Oh God, I thought, she's going around the group. Then I thought, if I stay in the bushes they won't see me.

One after another they "revealed" themselves. It was getting funny. Laurie is not going to believe this, I thought.

"I'm a home-loving person," Marcia Silver, dressed in a tight, black gown, was saying. She was the last to speak, since Frank and Susie were still in the bushes and Jason was with me.

"Well, that was really honest," Shelley exclaimed, wrapping up the group therapy session.

"Just a moment," Jason stepped forward.

I was disappointed. I was getting to like him and here he was playing Shelley's stupid game.

"You've forgotten someone—Ruth." And he pushed me forward. I didn't know what was happening, I was so shocked.

"Here's a really honest person—a seeker of truths. Listen to this." And then, he did it. It must've been to get back at Shelley. Like she was getting all the attention he wasn't or something. In a loud, clear voice, he read my poem. When he finished, he spat out, "Here's a true friend, Shelley," and stomped off.

Most people were bewildered by his performance and they didn't understand the poem anyway. They whispered among themselves until Shelley said in a voice that could freeze a dragon's breath, "Very nice, Ru-thie."

"I'm sorry," I mumbled and ran out into the street, cursing Jason, cursing Shelley, but most of all, cursing myself. I tripped a couple of times and made a few wrong turns until I finally got home. It wasn't until I was standing, sweating, on my doorstep that I realized now I'd

have to face my parents. I wiped my eyes, calmed myself, and knocked on the door. My mother answered.

"Ruthie, what are you doing here?" she shrieked, "What
happened? You're going to give me a heart attack."

I mumbled something about being all right.

My father, hearing the noise, charged in like a bull
moose, "What the hell do you think you're doing? I said
eleven o'clock."

"You're going to give your father a heart attack," Mom
yelled.

Gram came in, "What is it? Rootie, you all right?"

With my parents yelling and my grandma being con-
cerned, my coolness failed and I burst into tears and ran
to my room. I heard Mom getting hysterical, "My God,
did someone attack her? Those crazy actors. I knew. I
knew."

"I told you she shouldn't go, but you wouldn't listen.
As usual. Now you see. Nobody ever listens to me," Dad
hollered.

Gram tried to calm them, "Maybe she just upset."

"She's upset. What about me?"

While they continued yelling, Gram came upstairs.
"You all right, Rootie," she said quietly and put her arms
around me, which made me cry all over again. It passed
through my head that I've sure been crying a lot these
days.

"That girl thinks she's so smart, so grown-up. And you
never listen to me," I heard my dad yell.

"Please, Arthur, you're getting too excited," Mom was
yelling back.

"What happened?" Gram asked.

When I finally could talk, I told her everyone had ignored me and then I'd been insulted because of my costume. What really happened was too difficult to explain.
"They are children, yet," she said.

"Yes, babies," I sniffed.

"You a child too. Maybe just smarter."

"Yes, Grandma," I sighed.

"Go to bed."

My parents got quieter. Grandma must've told them my story. I heard them saying, "That snotty Sugarman kid, huh?" Just as I was falling asleep, I thought of two things. One was that I didn't know what I was going to tell Laurie. The other was that, in the long run, I'd rather have a family who yelled at me than people who tell other people how awful I am, like Ms. Sugarman and Jason do about Shelley.

7

"You did what!" Laurie shrieked in admiration when I told her the Sugarman saga (I must admit I spiced it up a bit). Laurie does that occasionally—shriek, that is. And I always wince when she does.

"Listen, it's not so great. I'm going to be Number 1 on the school shit list."

"Oh, so what. That's only temporary. When they think about what you wrote, you'll be a heroine. The unmasker of the Sugar Woman." That was her favorite bit of the poem.

"Don't be dumb. They didn't even understand it." Frankly, I wasn't sure Laurie had either.

"You always think people are stupid," she pouted.

"Skip it," I warned. She had touched a sore spot—

mainly because what she said is true. I don't give people much credit in the brain area—but then I don't think I'm so wrong about that. There was one of those uncomfortable pauses until Laurie said, "Is her brother gorgeous?"

"Oh, for God's sakes, he was a snake. Didn't you hear what he did?" I was in a very intolerant mood.

"Something wrong, Ruthie?" a smooth voice interrupted. It was Sylvia, Laurie's mom. Sylvia is a truly strange person. She is always wearing her pajamas, even in the middle of the day, and she's never even ill. She doesn't have a job, but she doesn't do much housework or cooking either. Mostly, she drinks coffee and watches T.V. in bed. Also, she's always telling me how she got 95 on her English final and got into a really great college and that she could've been a writer or an actress if she hadn't met Laurie's father, Hank, whom my parents say is henpecked. I hate that expression and I like Hank. He's very sweet. Besides, people get what they choose, don't they? I once told Sylvia she still could write or act if she really wanted to, but she gave me a dirty look that said, "A lot you know." Now when she talks about it, I keep my mouth shut. The other thing about her is that she is a neighborhood gossip. Which is why I didn't want her to find out about me and Shelley's party.

"No, Sylvia, just auditioning for a class play."

"Really? Well, if you're that convincing when you actually try out, I'm sure you'll get the part."

"Thanks."

"It seems awfully strange to me, though, having a class play in June. School's nearly finished. By the way, how was Shelley Sugarman's party?"

Is there no peace, I thought. "It was okay." That was lame.

"Really? Sally Sugarman seemed to think you went

home upset. And Shelley and Jason apparently had a huge fight—so loud that Florence Heisinger heard it— during which your name was mentioned."

Florence Heisinger, another old snoop. Now I was getting angry. The bitch. Laurie was mad too.

"It was nothing . . . ," I began.

"Lay off, Ma," Laurie blurted.

Sylvia looked at her coldly. "I'd appreciate it if you'd fix lunch, Laurie."

"We were going . . . ," she started to say.

"NOW." And Sylvia marched back to her bedroom.

"Gee, Ru, I'm sorry." Laurie turned to me miserably.

"It's not your fault."

We were silent. I felt like crying again.

"Let's continue The Dream, okay?"

"Sure." Laurie was a little surprised.

"I'm a struggling writer, trying to . . ."

"Wait a second, I didn't even win my Academy Award yet."

"Please, Laur, we'll do yours later." I must've looked really pathetic because Laurie just nodded. And then, as Mom would say, we were off and running.

8

This morning, Monday, was awful—just what I expected. People giving me cold looks and talking behind my back. Kravitz called on me in History when I was thinking about the whole mess, and I flubbed the answer. The whole class snickered. In English, which is my best subject, we were studying irony—an appropriate topic if I ever saw one. Ms. Spielberg, who's got this beautiful lined face with high cheekbones which tells you she's seen a lot, and who is my favorite teacher, was using this terrific Dorothy Parker poem. Ms. Spielberg told us a lot about Dorothy Parker and how she was witty and nasty/funny and said things about people such as Katherine Hepburn— "Her acting runs the gamut from A to B" and stuff like that. The poem we were studying goes like this:

RÉSUMÉ

Razors pain you;
Rivers are damp;
Acids stain you;
And drugs cause cramp.
Guns aren't lawful;
Nooses give;
Gas smells awful;
You might as well live.

I appreciated the sentiment—especially as I was contemplating suicide at the moment. Well, I wasn't really, but you know how you get to picturing people crying at your funeral and the nice things they'd say about you now that you're gone. Anyway, Ms. Spielberg asked Shelley to explain how the poem was ironic. Shelley smiled sweetly and, honest-to-God, said, "Ms. Spielberg, I think you should put that question to our class poet."

Ms. Spielberg asked curiously, "Who do you mean, Shelley?" She is used to all the kibbitzing we do and figures the best way to deal with it is to play it straight.

"Why, Ruthie. You should hear the poem she wrote about me."

The class screamed with laughter.

Ms. Spielberg looked at me. I bit my lip and looked back. My eyes probably gave me away because Ms. Spielberg just said, "Okay, Shelley, how about answering my question about irony?"

After class, she called me over. "You want to talk about it?" She is very direct.

There are only three people in this world I can talk to: Laurie, Grandma, and Ms. Spielberg. Funny, though, I can't talk to them about the same things. I poured everything out. All of it. Straight. No spicing it up this time at all.

"They're such snobs and phonies," I said. "I don't fit in at all."

"Ruthie, there's such a thing as being a snob to snobs. If you can see that they're phony, why not just go one step farther and rise above all that? People are snobbish and phony because they're afraid of something. You know that. What are *you* afraid of?"

I didn't understand what she meant exactly. That is, I didn't understand it in my head, but I sure did in my stomach. I answered very slowly, "I guess I have to figure that out."

"Don't be so depressed about it. We all do," she laughed. "By the way, when are you going to show me some of those poems you've written?"

"I have to pick out the ones I like best."

"Why don't you toss in some of the ones you detest too? Then we can talk about why some work, while the others don't."

"Okay. And thanks."

An impish look appeared in Ms. Spielberg's eyes. "Dorothy Parker would have appreciated your 'Sugar Woman' poem."

"You think so?"

"I wouldn't be surprised."

After that, the rest of today wasn't so awful.

Part Two

9

"Ruthie, you're not eating your dinner."

"Oh, for God's sakes, Ma, I'm performing tonight."

"So. What does that have to do with your dinner?"

"Mother, if I put any of this food in my stomach, I will throw up when I get on stage."

"What's wrong with my food?" I'll say this for Mom, she sure can be persistent.

"You noivous, Rootie?" Grandma asked.

"Yes, Gram, very." Now why is it if Mom had asked that I would've answered with something sarcastic like, "No, whatever gave you that idea?" but I'd never be that way with Grandma.

"Then you need a good dinner. You get nervous, you get faint. Got to keep your blood sugar up." Mom is always reciting health tips. She once told me she'd wanted to be a doctor, but ended up in business college because her three brothers came first. I wish she *had* become a doctor. Then she'd at least have her facts straight.

"Pearl, I just remember when you sing for audience. You eat no-ting. Rootie be all right."

"That was before we knew about . . . ," Mom began.

I interrupted, "Hey, Ma, when did you sing before an audience? You never told me."

"Didn't I?" Mom launched right into a memory, fortunately forgetting about blood sugar. "I used to sing a lot—a true mezzo, they called me."

"What's a mezzo?"

"A type of soprano. Doesn't sing really high—that's a coloratura." Her voice took on a different quality. It had lost its New York accent and was, well, more refined, confident. Like she'd taken diction lessons or something. I should mention that Mom sings a lot, while washing the dishes and stuff. But it's fooling-around singing. She never does a song straight through. I could always tell she had a good voice, but I didn't know she'd sung seriously.

"I gave a recital for the whole school. The music teacher and I sang a duet."

"Wow. What was it?"

"Bach, I think."

"Really?" My mother has never, to my knowledge, listened to Bach since I've been born. Unless she does it on the sly or something.

"Bet you didn't know your mother was a songbird," Dad said. As usual, he'd been sitting quietly reading the paper through dinner. "Bet you didn't know your old man can sing too," he grinned. That was a joke. He *always* sings. In fact, when I was little, I wouldn't go to sleep unless he sang to me. That's how I learned so many old songs. He was in a good mood. When he's in a good mood, he acts a little daffy. He broke into a rendition of "St. James' Infirmary":

"I went down to St. James' Infirmary
To see my baby there.
She was stretched out on a long, white table,
So pale, so cold, so fair."

"Please, Dad, I hate that song." He knows that song gives me the creeps, and he likes to tease me with it.

"It's a famous old song—a classic."

"Good, it can stay a classic—as long as I don't have to hear it. Mom, tell me more about your recital."

"Oh, there's nothing much to tell. It went well; everyone congratulated me. No one offered me a career, though."

"Just like boid, she sing," Gram smiled fondly.

"Know what my high school yearbook says, under my picture? 'O, she can sing the savageness out of a bear.' That's Shakespeare." And then Mom blushed. I couldn't believe it. She never talks much about her talents. Suddenly, I felt happy.

"That's really nice. Do you still have the book?"

"Yes, I do." She never throws anything away. Our basement is stacked with papers I wrote in the first grade, T.V.s that don't work, old, moldy dolls, broken lawn mowers, and photographs.

"Can I see it?"

"I'll have to dig it out." But she went straight to a little cabinet in the living room and took the book out. I could tell it is one of her treasures. "Of course styles were different then." She showed me the picture and I was amazed. Not because she was so different looking, but because she looked so much the same.

"A real tootsie," Dad said.

"You haven't changed much," I said.

"Oh come on," Mom tried to sound sarcastic, but her blush gave her away. "Now eat some dinner," she added hastily.

"Later." I smiled and dashed upstairs to practice the songs once more.

10

"Hi, Hank. Hello, Stuie," I said as I slipped into the car. Hank has never asked me to call him Hank, but it would sound awfully strange calling Laurie's mom Sylvia and her dad *Mr.* Stein.

"Hello, Ruthie. How's tricks?"

"We could use some tonight."

"Some what?"

"Tricks."

"I don't want to go," Stuie whined and fidgeted.

"Stay home then," Hank said calmly.

"Don't want to."

"Then go."

"Don't want to."

"Da–da!" a voice sang out. It was Laurie wearing a

floor-length flowered dress. It wasn't an ugly dress, but I thought we'd had all that out. When she got into the car, bumping me with her guitar case, I noticed she was wearing a light layer of makeup.

"Well, what do you think?"

"Lovely, princess," Hank said, and smiled. Not too many fathers could call their daughters "princess" and get away with it.

"Don't want to," said the broken record.

Laurie turned to me. "What's the matter? You look like I smell bad."

"It's just, well, look at us. Don't you see a . . . a . . . difference?"

"So?"

"We're supposed to be a team—not competitors. You look like you're off to a dance and I . . . I . . . look like I'm off to the races." Don't ask me where I got that from.

"They dress up for the races," Laurie pouted.

"Oh, skip it. Where's Sylvia?"

"Coming later—with a surprise."

"A surprise?"

"Yeah, I'm hoping it's these earrings I've been talking about for two weeks."

"Don't count on it," Hank said mysteriously. I looked at him. He seemed a little sad.

"What's that smell?" Stuie sniffed.

"It's perfume," Laurie replied.

"It stinks."

"Ignore him," I sighed.

"Dad, will you shut him up?"

"Shut up, Stuie," Hank said mildly.

"Want to rehearse?" I asked.

"No. It's bad luck."

"It is?"

"You shut up," Stuie bellowed.

"That's what Mom says—that and whistling in the dressing room."

Show biz again. I was annoyed. "Since when is it bad luck to rehearse before a performance?"

"It is on the *day* of the performance."

"Bullshit . . . oops, sorry, Hank."

"Ruthie said 'bullshit,' " Stuie sang.

"Shut up, Stuie. That's okay, Ruthie. It *is* bullshit."

"What do you know? Mom was the actress, not you," Laurie yelled in a nasty way. She can really be mean to Hank. Sometimes, she sounds just like Sylvia.

"I doubt I could ever have been an actress," Hank answered.

I giggled.

"Ha, ha, very funny," Laurie snapped.

"Come on. You've got opening night nerves," I teased.

"I do not. I'm perfectly calm."

"Sure. And I'm Annie Oakley."

"Annie Oakley! Where'd you get that from?"

We looked at each other and suddenly laughed. Hank joined in. Even Stuie began to giggle. By the time we arrived at school, we were hysterical.

"Better calm down or you won't be able to sing," Hank said.

"Sing! Who's going to sing?" Laurie choked.

"Croak is more like it," I added, punching her arm.

Then Stuie punched her and she slapped him. They nearly had a fight until Hank broke it up. Finally, we were able to leave the car and go backstage.

Backstage was a jumble of bodies and props. Balls and pins for Johnny the Juggler, as John Hansen called himself. I once called him Johnny the Jugular because he has big veins that stand out all over when he juggles. He sweats a lot too. And he has performed at *every* talent night since he was a freshman. Since he's now a senior, this is his eighth time. As he'll probably be left back, he'll be up there twice more, I guess. Unfortunately, he's a lousy juggler.

Seven guitar cases, a set of drums, amps, suitcases filled with makeup, batons, tap shoes, costumes, and stuff, and a huge false-bottom magic box Lonnie Robbins' rich parents had bought for his act littered the area.

"How many singers are there?" I asked.

"Hundreds, by the look of it."

"Oh, hell."

"Take it easy. Didn't you figure there would be?"

"But we're on eighth. By the time we come on, everyone will be sick of singing."

"Listen, lady, just think of how much better we are."

My nerves were giving way and I was beginning to chatter. When I get nervous, I talk a lot. And the more I talk, the quieter Laurie gets.

"Did you check your guitar?"

"Yes."

"It's in tune?"

"For God's sakes, Ruthie!"

"Okay."

Shelley Sugarman waltzed in with a professional-looking makeup kit, accompanied by Mitch.

"You think we have any chance of winning?" I asked.

"Well, there are four prizes, right?"

"Yeah, so?"

"So. We have a chance."

I didn't follow the logic.

"Five minutes," Lloyd Hertzberg shouted unnecessarily. Lloyd is the son of Mr. Eric Hertzberg, Math teacher and head of the Hosts, a club that ushers things. That's how he got to be stage manager. Anyway, the first act, Judy Thomas and her Twirling Baton, had been ready a half hour ago. Judy had gone through her routine three times already and was working on the fourth.

"Bad luck," I said, sauntering over to her.

"Huh?"

"It's bad luck to rehearse on the day of performance."

"This isn't daytime. It's night already." From someone else, this might have been clever, but not from Judy.

"Same thing." I acted dead serious.

"Oh go on," she squeaked. But I noticed she'd stopped twirling.

The show began. Judy, then Johnny the Jugular, then Lonnie, who really was a wonderful magician. We watched him from the wings. He was so good, we forgot about our nerves for a while. Next, The Druids, possibly the worst rock group I've ever heard. Only their name is interesting. Then, came the first of the Sugar People—Shelley's friends. Luanne Elkins appeared in a long dress, shook her long blonde hair, and sang two long Joni Mitchell songs.

"She's good," I moaned.

"She's nowhere as good as us. And her material isn't original," Laurie said confidently.

Intermission. Shelley and Mitch doing a scene from *Saint Joan* would follow. Then, Roz doing a tap dance. Then, a pair of singers I didn't know. Then, us.

"I saw my father and mother out there," Laurie bubbled.

"I never knew your parents were such a treat."

"There's somebody else with them," she sang.

"Of course—Stuie."

"Idiot. No, it's Harvey Traeger."

"Who the hell is Harvey Traeger?"

"He's a professional photographer. A friend of my uncle's. I met him once."

I got the picture slowly. "Your mother hired a professional photographer? What for?"

"What do you mean, 'what for?' I think it's really nice."

"This is a school talent contest!"

"So what! It would still be good for a portfolio or . . ."

"A portfolio! Are you still thinking about show biz?"

Laurie had no time to reply. A shrill voice cut in. "Ruthie! I heard you were performing, but I didn't believe it. Reciting a poem?" she emphasized in her hydrochloric acid voice. She just can't let go of that incident. Maybe she was shook up by it. I mean, it is a nasty poem, but it is also true.

"No, Shelley. Singing." I decided not to show my irritation.

"Shakespeare set to music?" she smirked.

"Better. My own lyrics." I smiled and walked away.

"Five minutes," Lloyd called again.

"Jerk," I muttered to Laurie. But she was too preoccupied. So, she is nervous, I thought. I had to talk to someone so I cornered Lonnie and talked magic with him until the curtain went up. He wouldn't tell me how anything was done, but he was surprisingly modest. I decided I like him. But he's a junior, so I doubt he's very interested in me.

Shelley and Mitch did their scene. For all of Shelley's reputation, no one had actually seen her act. I thought she was terribly overdramatic, but she got a huge hand. She curtsied like a prima donna. When Mitch bowed, his beard fell off. He turned red. The audience laughed. He picked up the beard and flung it to the first row. The audience applauded.

"First place," Shelley smiled at him when they exited.

"*Mais oui*," he played up to her.

Roz, in spangles and bowed tap shoes, went on and did her imitation bit. "Ginger Rogers," she announced and did what she thought was Ginger. "Ann Miller." "Ruby Keeler." "Eleanor Powell." Only the grown-ups knew who she was talking about—and me and Laurie because we watch so many old movie musicals. I guess Shelley knew too.

"And now—me," Roz grinned, going into her own routine, which I must admit was better than her imitations. She climaxed with a split that didn't fit, but got loud applause. I guess the adults felt nostalgic.

The two singers—Pat and Mike (both boys) came next. Pat was tall, thin, and goofy-looking. He had genuine red hair and was covered with freckles. Mike was just the opposite—short, dark, and heavy. I muffled a giggle. "What a pair!" Laurie blurted out.

"We'd like to do two of our own songs. The first is called 'Summer Blues,'" Mike said.

Summer Blues! Could you think of a duller name for a song, I thought. Then they started to sing. Damn, damn, damn. Not only were they good, but they even looked good. I guess that's what they mean when they say their art "transformed" them. I turned to Laurie. She looked defiant.

"They're . . . ," I began.

"Terrific," she finished. "That's why we're going to show 'em up."

"Huh?"

"I said we're going to show 'em up." She was positively fierce.

My stomach turned over. Laurie loves real competition. I hate it. "I've got to go to the toilet," I whispered.

"Hurry up," she ordered.

I fled. Once there, I contemplated not returning. Come on, Ruth, don't chicken now, Laurie will hate you for life. But I'll make a fool of myself out there. You'll be a bigger one if you don't go on, my head argued.

When I crept back, knees shaking, Laurie grabbed me, "We're on."

And we were—on, that is.

"Our first song, written by Ruth," Laurie announced, "is called 'Right Now.'"

The first line, what was the first line? I was frantic. All those faces. My parents and Grandma. Hank and Sylvia and Stuie and Harvey Traeger. Shelley Sugarman in the wings. I was going to blow it. Then, Laurie started playing and my mouth began to sing by itself as Laurie joined in with the harmony.

We exited to tremendous applause (Laurie said). I honestly can't remember. I also don't know who came after us. All I know is that Laurie was ecstatic and I raced for the toilet. I returned just in time for the awards.

"And now, I want to announce the prizes," Mr. Hertzberg said, and beamed.

We all huddled tensely backstage.

"There are four awards tonight. Third prize. Second prize. First runner-up. First prize."

Mr. Hertzberg is a boring teacher. He's also a boring host.

"The envelope, please."

Everyone tittered. Of course, there was no envelope.

"The judges have reached their decision."

The judges were Mr. Hertzberg, Ms. MacClean, a Gym teacher who pretended to teach dance, Ms. Madden, the Drama teacher (Brownie points for Shelley), and Mr. Weinstein, the Music teacher, who's crazy and lots of fun.

"Third prize is awarded to—Roz Schecter."

"Oh my God," Laurie said in disgust.

"Forget it," I murmured. I decided if she had won, we had no chance—it was novelty they were looking for.

Roz squealed, hugged Shelley, who looked like someone who's annoyed and trying not to show it, cartwheeled

on stage, and went into a split. Mr. Hertzberg helped her
up and gave her the plaque.

"Second prize goes to—Pat and Mike."

Laurie and I just looked at each other.

Pat and Mike clumped out and graciously accepted
their award.

"First runners-up are . . ."

By this time, Laurie and I were clutching each other.

"Laurie and Ruthie."

"It's us," Laurie yelled.

"My God," I gasped.

"Well, honestly," I heard Shelley snort.

We stumbled out, grinning like fools. The audience
swam before me as I smiled and bowed.

"First prize," Mr. Hertzberg was droning.

I heard him vaguely and remembered to look toward the
wings. Shelley was about to step forward.

". . . Lonnie Robbins."

Laurie poked me and I smiled until my face was ready
to crack.

After that, there was a rush of people to the stage. Hugging and kissing and stuff. Word passed that Shelley had
quickly disappeared, not even bothering to congratulate
Roz. In the excitement, Lonnie and I hugged each other.
I liked it.

"Ruthie, Laurie, you did it," my parents were saying.

"Like boids," Gram smiled.

"Wonderful, Laurie darling, Ruthie dear. Now could
you get closer," Sylvia was saying.

"A big smile." Harvey Traeger grinned broadly to show
us what we were supposed to look like.

"Now, Laurie alone. It's for her scrapbook," Sylvia emphasized for my benefit. Like I said, Sylvia is weird. But I
didn't really care too much about anything right then. I
was so pleased I just kept giggling and hugging.

"Sundaes?" my dad asked everyone gaily. He must have been really pleased because he almost never suggests that we go out, especially with the Steins.

"A fine idea." Hank beamed.

"Hank, I'm much too tired. Why don't we go home . . . Laurie and Stuie can go. Give them some money."

I know I'll never hear the end of that one from Mom tomorrow. Foisting Stuie off on my parents! But they were too happy to care right then.

"Oh come on, Syl," Hank squeezed her.

"I said I'm *tired*."

Everyone went quiet.

"All right," Hank finally said sadly. I felt a pang of pity for him. He looked so disappointed. But then we all started talking again and bustled out into the parking lot.

"And here they are, the hottest singing team in New York," Dad said as we reached the car.

"New York? The East Coast," I said.

"The East Coast? The U.S.A.," Laurie said, and laughed.

"North America."

"The Northern Hemisphere."

"The World."

"The Universe."

"Oy vay," Gram shook her head.

We all laughed.

"I want a banana split," Stuie yelled.

"How about a split lip?" Laurie yelled back.

"Hey, Laur," I asked when we were in the Howard Johnson's toilet, "You think your mom was really tired?"

"Sure. Why not?"

"Oh, nothing." But I remembered Sylvia's face when Harvey Traeger finished snapping his pictures. She looked just the way Shelley did when Roz Schecter won. I decided not to mention it to Laurie, though. I had a feeling it would upset her.

11

Sylvia was in bed with a headache. Hank was mowing the lawn. Stuie was off somewhere, thank God. And Laurie and I were making plans for the future.

"We ought to tape everything."

"Sure," I said.

"If we made a good tape, we could send it around."

"To whom?"

"You know—recording companies."

"Oh yeah. They're all looking for a girl duo who almost won the school talent contest to promote."

"Why not? That's unique."

"You're nuts," I yawned. "Let's continue The Dream."

"No, I want to figure this out. People make it big. There's no reason we can't."

"Oh no?"

"Name three reasons."

"No contacts. No money. No experience. And we're fourteen. That's four reasons."

"Fourteen is unique. I already told you that. We can get experience. Our parents could put up the money."

"Ha!"

"And my mother is real good at making contacts."

I'll bet she is, I thought, she just has to pick up the phone on her night table and dial. But aloud, I said, "Yeah? She know any theatrical agents?"

"Probably," she said stubbornly.

"Ask her to fix us up with an appointment."

"Okay. I will. You wait and see."

"Fine. Now can we continue The Dream. I'm up for the Nobel Prize. . . ."

"I didn't win my Academy Award yet."

"Okay. Okay."

"My mom thinks it's a good idea," Laurie said later, on the phone.

"What is?"

"To get a theatrical agent."

"Oh."

"She's going to start looking. . . ."

"How's her headache."

"Huh? Fine. Why?"

"Nothing."

"She also thinks I should get my hair done."

"What?"

"What's wrong with that?"

"What's wrong with your *hair*?"

"Don't act stupid. It's . . . it's passé." She must've gotten that from Sylvia. It sounded so silly I started to laugh.

"Jerk!" Laurie yelled and hung up.

Half an hour later she called me back to tell me she was going to start voice lessons—Sylvia's idea. She was very excited. All I said was, "That's nice," coolly.

Sometimes, she's almost as weird as Sylvia.

12

Suddenly, I'm not class turd anymore. Roz shook my hand. Luanne said she never knew I sang—and she didn't mean that in a nasty way. Even Mitch nodded at me. Shelley was conspicuously absent.

I had lunch with Pat and Mike, who are really nice guys. Laurie couldn't join us because she was taking a Math retest (she flunked the last one because it was on the day of the contest; her teacher's a creep). She told him she'd rather give up lunch than stay after school. Maybe that would make old Korfein see her as self-sacrificing, she said.

Mike showed me his latest lyrics. I suggested a few changes. He agreed. Then, Lonnie joined us. He and Pat and Mike are all friends. Lonnie teased me a lot.

"I could use an assistant. You know, someone to distract the audience."

"What would you want me to do—come out nude?"

"Now that you mention it . . ."

"Chauvinist!"

"It was your idea."

I know after the excitement and prestige of our winning wears off, I probably won't see them much, but I'm sure enjoying myself now.

In class, my teachers congratulated me. Ms. Spielberg gave a special wink.

"You and your friend were very good," she said after class.

"Thanks."

"Planning on a singing career?"

"I doubt it." I paused. "Actually, I think Laurie is."

"Oh?"

"She's about to start singing lessons. And I think her mother is agent-hunting."

"That's too bad. You may lose a good friend."

"You mean if she makes it?"

"No, I wasn't thinking in terms of her succeeding. It's even easier to lose someone who's *trying* to make it."

"Really?" I couldn't think of anything else to say.

"I have a feeling you're going to have to be a good friend to Laurie. You're going to have to put up with a lot."

I walked slowly to my next class, thinking about Ms. S.'s prediction. Someone bumped me. It was Laurie.

"No hello?" She was cheerful.

"Hello."

"Can't see you tonight."

"How come?"

"Singing lesson."

"Already?"

"Yep. See you tomorrow."

I sighed. It looks like Ms. Spielberg may be right.

13

Today, Laurie was absent from school. Laryngitis. Shelley
Sugarman, however, has returned. I was sitting with Lonnie, Pat, and Mike when she sauntered over.

"I never got a chance to tell you how good you were,"
she oozed.

"Thank you. Feeling better?"

"Pardon?"

"You've been absent."

"Oh yes. Much. Well, I must be going." She didn't move.

"Aren't you the girl who did *Saint Joan?*" Lonnie asked.

"Yes, I'm Shelley," she bubbled.

"Nice job."

My stomach knotted.

"Oh, I'm glad you liked it. . . . Ruthie, why don't you

introduce me to your friends?" To my disgust, she sat down.

"Pat, Mike, Lonnie," I mumbled.

"You all performed, didn't you? That magic act, how did you . . . ?" And she wiggled her way into a conversation with Lonnie.

I started to leave. Then, as an afterthought, I turned and said, "You know what, Shelley?"

She looked up.

"You have a good chance of turning out to be another Sylvia Stein."

"Is that good?" she asked.

"It depends on your definition of 'good.'" And I stomped off.

When I left school, I ran into Lonnie. "Hey, why'd you leave?" he asked.

"Leave?"

"Lunch. That Shelley was an awful bore."

"Lonnie, you have just made my day. See you tomorrow."

I've given a lot of thought to what Ms. Spielberg said about not being snobbish to snobs and I've decided in Shelley's case, it won't work.

I was dying to tell Laurie what happened. But when I got to her house, Sylvia answered the door.

"Ruthie, you know Laurie has laryngitis. She is not allowed to talk."

"I'll talk. She can just listen."

"Sorry, Ruthie. No."

"Do you think she'll be better tomorrow?"

"Probably, but she's going to have her hair done."

I almost swore. "I can see her after."

"It may take awhile."

I was furious. It seemed like Sylvia was trying to stop me from seeing Laurie. I never figured she liked me a lot, but this was too much. I took a deep breath. "Would you have her call me when she's finished?"

"Certainly . . . Oh, and Ruthie, I'm sure you'll be surprised when you see her."

I bet I will, I thought.

"Why don't you have yours done too?" She looked disapprovingly at my head.

"I prefer the natural look."

"Yes, but sometimes that doesn't always look good."

"Sometimes it doesn't," I said staring at her hair all tousled from lying in bed.

"Good-bye, Ruthie," Sylvia said icily, closing the door in my face.

Laurie hasn't called. But Lonnie has. He's asked me if I want to come over and see the film his dad took of the show. I was really excited and decided I'd be big about it and call Laurie. She was still having her hair done.

After that, I wasn't as excited. I mean, I suppose I should be delighted that Lonnie asked me, but I sort of counted on sharing the fun.

It's times like this I wish I had a sister. Mom had a baby before me, but she died. She was born dead. She's buried in the family plot, next to my grandfather. There's a small stone with BABY ZEILER engraved on it. It makes me a little sad, but more curious than anything else. She would've been my older sister. Maybe she would've been a good friend. Madeleine Minsky once told me her sister was her best friend. I didn't believe her at the time, but now I can see how it might be true. I mean, I like boys, but I need a real girl friend. Something Ms. Rising Celebrity Stein is not being at the moment. What's worse is that Mom is doing her I-told-you-so number again and also the fact that it's gotten around school that Laurie is taking singing lessons. If one more person asks me when I'm going to start them, I'll scream.

Tonight, I'm going to see that film at Lonnie's house. I am not going to try calling Laurie again today. She can call if she wants to. I intend to forget about her when I'm at Lonnie's, which will be a little difficult because we're both in the film. Anyway, at least Shelley won't be there. She wasn't invited.

14

"I've got a surprise. Can I come over?" Laurie giggled into the phone.

"All right," I said coolly.

Only Gram was home, so my parents couldn't make remarks about it afterwards.

She was here almost immediately. When Gram answered the door, I heard her exclaim, "My gootness!"

I ambled downstairs. My mouth dropped open. Laurie stood there, her once straight hair frizzled all over her head, her eyebrows tweezed to thin lines. She waved her hands at me—the nails were filed to sharp points and painted.

"You bite your nails," was all I could say.

"These are fake—until mine grow in underneath."

"Oh."

"Well?"

"I went to Lonnie's last night."

"*Ruthie,* what do you think of me?"

I wanted to yell that it was awful, ugly, I hated it. It wasn't Laurie. But I knew that would drive her away, maybe permanently. "I . . . ah . . . have to get used to it."

That seemed to satisfy her. "It is different, isn't it? Listen, I can't stay. I've got a singing lesson."

"But . . . ," I began.

"Tomorrow. We'll get together tomorrow." And off she went. She never even asked me about Lonnie's, where I had a really good time.

I sank into our shabby old couch and said nothing. Gram came over.

"She got bug."

I looked at my dirty fingernails. "No, it was only laryngitis."

"Not that kind bug. Hollywood bug."

I looked at her, "How do you know, Gram?"

"Photos. Singing lessons. Fan-cy hair-do. Oy vay."

"Gram," I said seriously, "what should I do?"

"What can you do? Wait. And try not to get angry. She got more problems than you."

Sometimes Gram reminds me of Ms. Spielberg. I should wait. But the thing is school's almost finished and now the summer, which I've been looking forward to, doesn't seem very inviting. For years I've spent my summers with Laurie. Sylvia always tried to pack her off to camp. Once she actually went for two weeks, got a case of hives from something in the food, and came home. Sylvia still didn't give up trying, but Laurie just told her not to waste her money. I've never been to camp at all. My parents have always told me how the food is bad, the bugs are rotten, the woods are full of snakes and poison ivy, and how I'm not athletic anyway. However, neither of my parents have ever *been* to camp. Anyway, Laurie and I always had so much fun swimming in her plastic pool or mine, singing, taking long walks with the heat rising from the asphalt just so we could experience the intense pleasure of Cokes in an air-conditioned candy store, and, of course, doing The Dream, that I never cared about camp. But this summer, what is there to look forward to? Waiting. Unfortunately, I'm a poor waiter. I thought about getting a job, but who'd hire a fourteen-year-old? I look even younger!

I got really depressed thinking that way this afternoon. Time for Emily D., I thought. But Gram had other ideas.

"Rootie, we bake challah. I teach you braiding."

"Challah! It's too warm for baking, Gram."

"Never too warm for challah. Come."

Many times I've watched her make the dough, and then, when it was ready, to pound and knead and stretch it into long ropes which she braided and brushed with butter and baked. I've always wanted to learn how, but Mom said, "Wait until you're older." Gram pooh-poohed her, but she insisted. I think because her challahs never turned out as good as Gram's and she was afraid mine might be.

We spent hours working on the breads and by the time they were in the oven, I was floury and happy.

"Bread cures heart," Gram said.

"Better than chicken soup?"

"That for belly, not heart," she said, and laughed.

And so did I.

15

"Look, tell him I'm sick or something. You can do that."

"He's your uncle. He has invited us over. I don't understand why you don't like him. He's always brought you presents. Remember that wonderful Rags-to-Riches doll? That kitchen set? That . . ."

Oh God. Why can't Mom see I'm not six anymore? Every time Uncle Sol invites us, I have to come along even though I'm always grumpy afterwards, having had a perfectly awful time.

"A string of cultured pearls," she was still going on.

"They were simulated. Fake. You don't know the difference," I snapped.

"Don't you snap at me. Get dressed," she yelled and stalked off.

I kicked a chair leg, hurt my toe, and limped to my room. Laurie was free today and now I couldn't even see her. I started to dress slowly. Mom won't let me wear jeans to Sol and Claire's because they live in a big, fancy house in Westchester. The living room has a chandelier, a grand piano which no one plays, and chairs with satin upholstery. Mom doesn't think jeans go with the furniture.

I tried every way I knew how to get out of going. I said I had exams coming up. Mom said we'd only be there for a few hours and I could study when we got back. I said I had a headache. She gave me two aspirins. Oh well, I decided, I'd bring along Emily, a pad of paper, and a crossword-puzzle book. That should keep me occupied.

Cousin Bernard's friend Mort Schumsky was having lunch with us; he's in town for a week and thought Bernard would be around, but Bernard and Gail are cruising in the Bahamas. Mort Schumsky is a pale, quiet man who stutters. He is also very rich. I suspect that is why Uncle Sol invited him to stay the week. He sat and laughed at Sol's lame jokes and then went down to play pool with Dad and Sol. Aunt Claire was busy cooking (she only cooks when we come—her housekeeper does it the rest of the time). Mom and Gram were helping.

Lunch was worse than turkey. Big, thick, rare steaks oozing red all over the platter. My stomach jerked. And I can't stand big lunches anyway. Aunt Claire started to serve Mort first.

"No, th-th-th-th-th-thanks," he said quietly.

"Anything the matter, Mort?"

"I'm a v-v-v-v-v-veget-t-t-tarian."

"Well, for goodness sakes, why didn't you tell me? I could've made something else," she said, flustered.

"N-n-no need. I'll eat the-the-the s-s-s-salad and v-v-v-v-vegetables."

No one said anything else about it.

When Aunt Claire reached me, I said, "I'm a vegetarian too."

"What's this nonsense?" Dad warned.

"Since when?" Mom added.

Gram was quiet, but she looked confused.

"I'm trying it out. It makes you feel good, doesn't it, Mr. Schumsky?"

"M-m-m-ort. S-s-s-ure does. You d-d-don't f-f-feel g-guilty about all those c-cows," he finished proudly.

Dead silence. Mort Schumsky had said the wrong thing. But I was delighted.

After dinner, Sol snoozed, Claire, Mom, and Gram did the dishes, and Dad played solitaire. I walked in the garden with Mort.

"What do you do?" I asked him.

"I'm in the b-book b-binding b-business. Sol s-sells me p-p-paper."

"Is it interesting?" I wondered how come he was rich. His family, probably.

"N-not v-very. W-what do you d-do?"

"I'm in school. I want to be a writer. Or a singer."

"You ha-ha-have an agent?" He seemed dead serious. I looked at him curiously. How old did he think I was?

"No. Know any?" I kidded.

"Yes, as a m-m-matter of f-fact. My b-b-brother. He's a theatrical agent."

Wow, this was unreal. "Think he'd listen to my friend and me? We're a duo."

"M-m-m-maybe as a f-f-favor. B-b-but not otherwise."

I liked Mort Schumsky. He was blunt. But, probably nobody pays much attention to him because he stutters. Maybe that's why he can be blunt.

"I'll ask him," he added.

"Gee, thanks a lot." I got very excited. Wait'll I tell Laurie I found us an agent, I thought. Then, I decided I'd better hold off until it was clear he'd listen to us.

"G-g-give me your ph-ph-phone n-n-n-n-number and I'll c-c-c-call," he swallowed hard, "you tonight. I'm s-s-seeing him l-later," he added.

"Thanks a lot, Mort."

"Anything f-for a f-fellow v-v-vegetarian," he smiled shyly.

When we got into the car, my parents lit into me.

"What is this vegetarian business?"

"You hurt Claire's feelings."

Even Gram added, "Rootie, you eat no meat, you get sick." In some ways, she's old-fashioned.

No one could hurt Aunt Claire's feelings, I thought. She has none. But I knew they'd get furious if I said it and also, I was really excited about Mort's brother. So I just said that my science teacher had said that meat is very hard to digest and would they like me to get them a book on the subject.

"Hard to digest?" Mom muttered. Like I said, she's a real sucker for statistics.

"High cholesterol and stuff. I'll get you the book."

They dropped the subject. I sat back and planned how I would tell Laurie we had an audition.

I refrained from calling Laurie all evening and was squirming with anticipation.

At ten o'clock, the phone rang. I rushed for it.

"H-hello, R-Ruthie?"

"Yes, Mort?"

"It's ok-k-kay. H-he's free at n-n-nine o'clock, T-T-Tuesday evening."

"Really? Wow. That's great, Mort!"

"His name is Lawrence Simpson. It w-was S-Sam Schumsky, b-but he ch-ch-changed it. Better for business," he added dryly. Then, he gave me the address.

"We'll be there. Thanks a lot."

After I hung up, I hurriedly dialed Laurie's number. Stuie answered.

"Who is it?"

"Ruthie, you misfit. Is Laurie there?"

"We don't want any."

"You'll get plenty if you don't call her to the phone."

A long couple of minutes passed. Then Laurie said, "Hi, Ruthie. How were Claire and Solly?"

"The same," I said casually. "What did you do today?"

"Practiced singing. Washed my hair. I've got big news, though."

"Yeah?"

"Ready. Mom's buying me a piano."

"A piano!"

"Yeah, to accompany me."

"But you play guitar."

"Well, this is to work on singing."

I failed to see the logic. "Listen, I've got some news too."

"You don't sound very pleased about my piano." I could hear her pouting.

"It's terrific. Now, you want to hear my news?"

"Okay," she grouched.

"I met a guy named Mort Schumsky at Sol and Claire's," I began, savoring the story.

"Was he cute?"

"He was adorable," I cooed, trying not to giggle. "And we got to talking." I paused dramatically.

"Well, go on." Laurie was getting interested.

"It appears his brother is an agent—a theatrical agent."

"What!"

"And it also appears we have an audition on Tuesday night, nine o'clock," I finished triumphantly.

"Aaaaeeeee!" screamed Laurie. Then, "Where is it? What's his name? You'd better get your hair done. We've got to rehearse."

"It's in Manhattan. Lawrence Simpson. I will not. We'll rehearse tomorrow night."

"Yippee. Wait'll I tell Mom."

It wasn't until after I hung up that I realized (a) I have a final exam in History on Wednesday; (b) we live thirty miles from Manhattan. Bad news, I thought, there's no way Mom and Dad will let me go. I pondered awhile. Then it struck me that this time, Sylvia might actually come in handy.

16

"Do you have to wear that? What kind of impression do you want to make?" Mom fussed.

"Oh, Ma, this is a perfectly respectable outfit," I said, tugging at the sleeve of my Indian top.

"An audition—and you're wearing pants!"

"Yep. And that's what I'll be wearing when I perform too."

I don't know how much my mother really cared about what I was wearing. When she gets nervous, she has to have something to fuss about.

"I hope that Sylvia gets you home by eleven o'clock. You're going to be in some fine shape for that exam tomorrow."

I mumbled something about it being at noon and how I

was well-prepared. I'd already told her that, but I figured I might as well humor her.

I was right about Sylvia. Laurie has an exam tomorrow too, but that doesn't mean nearly as much to Sylvia as a singing career for her daughter. She worked it all out— telling Mom she'd drive us there and hustle us back by eleven, and that Laurie has an exam too and why not just make sure we study Monday night and Tuesday (neither of us had exams on Tuesday), leaving, of course, an hour each day for rehearsal. Sylvia was—and is—very glib, not that it mattered that much—almost anyone can convince Mom of anything, except me.

All the way to the audition, I chattered, as usual, and Laurie was quiet, as usual. At one point, Sylvia said, "Ruthie, you're going to lose your voice at this rate."

"I doubt it," I answered. She was being snide, but I was too nervous to care.

We got to West Fifty-fifth Street and, miraculously, found a parking place. The street was grubby. A drunk staggered past us on his way to who knows what. A movie theater showing *Sex Life in the Ozarks* was next to the building we entered. And the building itself was gray and musty, part warehouse, part studios. At least, that's what I gathered from the directory. We rode up in a creaky elevator. I was sure it was going to stop between floors and, with all the padding in it, nobody would hear us yelling. But it didn't stop. When we got out at the fifth floor, I held the door open for an incredible-looking blonde woman in a slinky pants suit. She was saying, " 'Bye, Larry, and thanks." Already I didn't like Mr. Simpson.

"Come on, girls," Sylvia tugged me away from the elevator. She charged in ahead of us. I heard her say, "Mr. Simpson, this is so kind of you," before I even saw him. And when I did see him, I wasn't prepared. He was tall, solid, with a mass of carefully styled graying hair. He wore a handsome tan suit and had an enormous smile. His teeth are capped, I thought, looking at his gleaming choppers. He looked nothing like Mort Schumsky. And I got the feeling he was glad about that.

"So, you're going to sing for me?" he asked Sylvia.

Sylvia giggled. It was an Oh-Mr.-Simpson-Really giggle and it was truly awful. "No, my daughter, Laurie, and her friend, Ruthie, are the singers."

"My brother said to expect two girls, but here's three," he flashed his teeth. The song "Never Smile at a Crocodile" passed through my head.

Sylvia giggled again. I made a puke face at Laurie and she slapped my arm. Sylvia glanced at us.

"Mort seems to think you're good, so let's hear you."

"Mort never . . . ," I began.

"Oh, he's absolutely correct," Sylvia interrupted. "Ready, girls?"

Laurie picked up her guitar. I stood next to her. She started to play the introduction and her fingers slipped. I winced. "Excuse me, I'll start again," she said.

And we sang.

And Sylvia beamed.

And Mr. Simpson applauded. "Very, very nice."

"You'll be our agent?" I blurted out. I hadn't meant to— I was just so nervous. Laurie poked me.

"Well now, Laurie, I really don't know yet."

"Ruthie."

"Beg your pardon?"

"I'm Ruthie. This is Laurie." Sylvia, her back to Mr. Simpson, gave me a horrible look.

"Oh. Well, as I was saying, it takes time for me to decide. Can't just make a snap decision, can we? Just give me your phone numbers and I'll call and let you know."

Don't call us, we'll call you. Isn't that the way they always get rid of people?

"When do you think you'll know, Mr. Simpson?" Sylvia asked.

"Oh—in a few days," he winked at her.

Sylvia thanked him profusely. He shook her hand. I noticed he kept holding it for a few minutes after they stopped speaking. Laurie gave him her "winning smile." I said nothing.

"Ruthie, you must learn the right things to say to these people," Sylvia reproached when we got to the car.

"Did you say the right things?" I retorted.

"What do you mean?"

"Do you think you convinced him to be our agent?" I said more politely.

"I don't know about that, but *I* didn't muff my lines."

"What lines?" Laurie asked sleepily.

"Just an expression, Laurie."

"He certainly seemed to like us," I said.

"Yes . . . Laurie, you've never sounded better."

"Mmmm," she sighed. She hadn't slept at all last night.

"And you looked marvelous. Ruthie dear, if he does call, try to wear something different next time."

I gritted my teeth. "It's nice to see *you* in street clothes." That is possibly the rudest thing I've ever said in my life, but I couldn't help it. I was tired and fed up. Mr. Simpson is a creep and Sylvia can't stand me. Laurie wasn't even defending me; she was asleep.

"Why, you . . . ," Sylvia began.

"Look out," I yelled as she nearly crashed into the truck ahead of us. She is a terrible driver.

For the rest of the ride home, we were all quiet.

17

Exam time is always crazy and this one is crazier than most. Before today's exam, I rushed into the toilet. Shelley Sugarman was sitting on the floor, shakily trying to light a cigarette. Her face was white.

"Wanna cigarette?" she slurred.

"No, thanks."

"You don't smoke, do you?"

"No."

"Not grass either."

"How did you know that?"

"Jason told me. Do you take any drugs?" Her tone was strange, unsteady.

"No. Hey, are you okay?"

"Sure." She leaned her head against the wall.

"It's time for the exam."

"Listen, could you . . . er . . . give me a hand?"

"Huh?"

"Help me up."

I stuck out my hand. Shelley grabbed it and teetered to her feet. She turned to the sink and washed her face.

"You sure you're okay?"

"Yes—ummppp." With that, she bolted into a stall and threw up. Loudly. If there's anything that makes me sick, it's people puking. But even then, my nasty mind managed to think, My God, Shelley Sugarman actually vomits, like real people do. Then, I wanted to leave. Still, I knew I couldn't just abandon her. "You want me to tell Kravitz you're sick?"

"I'll be all right," she said when she finished. Then, she washed her face again and rinsed her mouth. "Jason gave me a pill last night so I could stay up and study. He swore it wouldn't make me sick, the swine. Oh, my gut." For once, she sounded like a normal fifteen-year-old.

"Did you get any sleep?"

"No."

"That's probably why you're sick."

The bell rang.

"We've got to go," I said.

"Listen, Ruthie, do me a favor. Just forget about this. I'll return the favor. Okay?"

"You don't have to. I won't tell anyone."

"Thanks. Look, I'll send you some tickets for the play I'm in this summer."

Big favor. What about the fare to Cape Cod and a place to stay? But what I said was "Sure."

By the time we got to the exam, Shelley had fixed a smile on her face for Kravitz and I got yelled at for being late, but frankly, I didn't care. I discovered that Shelley Sugarman is human.

The exam itself wasn't bad except there was a big question about serfs and fiefs and vassals—stuff we spent exactly one day discussing. I almost wrote "We are the serfs of Lord Kravitz and we are rebelling," but I restrained myself. I finished a bit early and had a daydream. I was walking around a fairy-tale castle eating gingerbread. I was three years old. When I woke up, I was sorry to find myself eleven years older, sitting in a classroom. I really went to a place called Gingerbread Castle when I was little. It is somewhere in New Jersey. I'm glad other people can't see your daydreams because I'd have been pretty embarrassed by that one, even though I enjoyed it.

"H-h-hello, R-R-Ruthie. This is M-M-M-M-Mort. H-how did it go-go?"

"Hi, Mort. Okay, I guess. Did you speak to your brother?"

"N-no. I thought I'd g-g-get the rep-p-p-pport from you."

"He said he'd let us know in a few days."

"That's the way h-h-he usually w-works."

"That's good to know." I didn't want to tell him about Sylvia.

"D-did he fl-fl-flirt?"

"Excuse me?"

"H-h-he prides himself on s-s-success with ladies!"

I didn't know what to say. "A little," I finally admitted.

"It f-figures. Anyway, h-how w-w-would you and your friend like to c-c-come to the b-beach on S-S-S-Saturday morning? I'm l-leaving on S-S-Sunday and I'd l-like to s-see you b-before I g-g-go."

"I'd love to. I'll ask Laurie and my parents and call you back."

My parents thought it was "sweet of him." As I was about to call Laurie and ask her, the phone rang.

"Speak of the devil," I said.

"Huh?" Laurie asked.

"Nothing. Do you want to come to the beach on Saturday morning with Mr. Simpson's brother?"

"Maybe."

"Maybe? I thought you love the beach."

"Yeah, but I may have to go somewhere with my parents. Listen," she added quickly, "you want to have dinner here Friday night?"

"Your parents going out?"

"No."

Let me say that Laurie almost never invites me for dinner when her parents are in. Furthermore, considering the note on which Sylvia and I parted last night, I can't imagine why she'd want me over. "How come?" I asked.

"Mom thinks we should celebrate."

"Celebrate what? Hey, Simpson didn't call, did he?"

"What makes you think that?" Laurie's voice cracked.

I had a funny feeling, but I didn't ask any more questions. I've got three more exams to get through and I don't want to have a nervous breakdown before them. Anyway, maybe it's just my fertile imagination.

"Mom just wants to celebrate our first audition."

"Oh. Okay," I said, "I've got to study. See you Friday."

When I hung up, I had a weird urge to look up the word "friend" in the dictionary:

FRIEND (frend). n. 1. a person attached to another by feelings of affection or personal regard. 2. a person who gives assistance; a patron or supporter: *a list of friends of the Boston Symphony.* 3. one who is on good terms with another; one not hostile: *to identify oneself as friend or foe; a cat and dog who are not friends.*

Sometimes I think Laurie's definition of friend is—one who is not hostile. If she looked in the dictionary, she'd see that there are more important definitions that come before hers.

18

"I don't know what's wrong with the world. It's just falling apart. Someone else jumped off the George Washington Bridge. Only twenty-eight years old too. 'Paul Harris.' Could be Jewish."

"They're laying off some more men in my shop."

"Did you know that the Michaels boy was involved in a robbery? Right around the block."

"It's a good thing I have some seniority. But even that doesn't count for much nowadays."

"You want I should make fish tonight?"

"They broke into the zoo again and killed a . . ."

"Ma, please," I yelled. I had been very quiet over breakfast, thinking about the day's exams and Laurie's invitation. Usually, I can shut off a lot of their conversations—if you can call them that—but not today. I don't know why

Mom always goes on about catastrophes, major and minor. It's either that or who's getting married or divorced or pregnant. And my dad—he's always worried about his job. He's a stripper, which sounds like a weird profession for a man, but actually it has to do with printing. Once, when I was little, I went to visit him in his shop. There were big machines all over the place; they smelled both greasy and sour, like some kind of acid. To this day, I don't quite understand what he does.

"So what exams do you have today?" Once again, Mom zapped right into another subject. And she knew perfectly well what exams I had.

"Science and English," I answered anyway.

"Did you study enough?" Dad asked.

"I think so."

"Your last one's tomorrow?"

"Yeah. Math." I made a face.

"I don't understand why you hate Math. It was my best subject. I wanted to be a civil engineer, you know."

"Yes, I know. Only you couldn't afford college after awhile." That was about the twentieth time he'd told me that.

"Listen, she's a girl," Mom broke in. "Girls are almost always bad in Math."

"For God's sakes . . . ," I began. She's always telling me what girls are good and bad at.

"Rootie, how's Laurie?" Grandma interrupted. She knows how to prevent an argument.

I paused, then said, "Fine. Oh, by the way, I've been invited there for dinner tomorrow night."

"Hank and Sylvia going out?"

"No."

"What! What's the occasion?"

"To celebrate our audition." I tried to be convincing.

"I thought we'd all go to the movies tomorrow night. There's that bank robbery picture," Dad said.

"But, Arthur, you said we could see the other film. The one with that new actress, what's her name?" Mom whined.

"You know I can't stand her."

"Arthur, for once. . . ."

"I've got to go. I'll be late," I said.

They were still arguing when I left.

My Biology exam was pretty fair. At lunch, I looked for Laurie. She wasn't around. That was strange because she'd promised to meet me and then split (she had only one exam, in the morning).

Lonnie trotted in. I hadn't seen him since exams started. He plopped into the seat next to mine.

"Hey, sweetie. Wanna come to my place and see my tricks?" he said in his W. C. Fields voice.

"What do you have up your sleeve?" I retorted.

"Actually, my old man bought me some doves."

"Really?" I was excited. I love birds. "Can I see them?" I asked without thinking.

But Lonnie was pleased. "Sure, how about Saturday night? I'm holding a performance in my salon."

"Huh?"

"My living room."

"Oh. Sure."

"Bring any friends you'd like."

"Sure." Damn, I was hoping it was a private performance. But you can't have everything. "Hey, Lonnie. What're you doing this summer?"

"My parents own a house in Cape Cod. We always go there."

"Yeah? Then you can see Shelley perform."

"I wouldn't miss it," he snorted.

"She's sending me tickets."

"I didn't think you were on such good terms."

I remembered my promise to her and just shrugged.

"Well, if you need a place to stay, you'd be welcome at our house."

Had I been pushing for that? I couldn't believe it. I wanted to shout, "I'll stay all summer." But I just thanked him and said I'd write if I were coming. And I most certainly will be coming!

The English exam was fun—as much fun as any exam can be. Believe it or not, we had to discuss an Emily Dickinson poem. I'm sure I did well on that. I had a bit of time before I could leave, so I wrote a parody of a rock song. At least, *I* think it's a parody. Actually, it might be fun to sing. It goes:

> Hothouse flower
> > Never seen the sun.
> Ain't been face-washed with rain,
> > Ain't got nowhere to run.
> A city girl
> > Don't know about the real world.
> Hothouse flower
> > Never seen the sun.
>
> Sprayed carnation—
> > No color of her own,
> Never been bee-kissed
> > Or been left alone.
> A city girl
> > Don't know about the real world.
> Hothouse flower
> > Never seen the sun.

I figured I'd suggest it to Laurie when I called to find out why she didn't meet me today. We could definitely use more material in our repertoire. Maybe a new slant would get us an agent. I've decided it's mean of me not to trust Laurie. And I've also decided not to count on Mr. Simpson. I just wish this weird feeling that something's wrong would go away.

I called Laurie's house. Hank answered. He said that Laurie and Sylvia had gone out on an errand and would be back late, which is odd, because she's got two exams tomorrow.

I wonder if I should go to camp this summer.

19

We had just moved into the neighborhood. I was five years old. I remember playing War with some rough kids. The victims, which included myself, crouched in a big box which the Enemy pelted with rocks. The box tilted, I slipped and got a bloody nose. Crying, I tried to go home and found I had lost my house. A kindly neighbor finally steered me home. After that, I stayed away from the wild kids. That's how I became friends with Laurie. She was one of the few children even more timid than I was. I saw her standing on her lawn, so I boldly trotted over and introduced myself. Laurie told me years later she had been terrified of me—I seemed so confident. How can someone you've been friends with for almost ten years betray you the way Laurie did to me tonight?

My eyes hurt. I guess they're pretty swollen.

My parents want to know what's wrong. I'm not letting them in my room.

The day started off rotten too. That Math exam was even harder than I expected. I probably failed, which means I'll have to go to summer school and be stuck in this stinking town. How the hell can Shelley Sugarman be taking Honors Math?

I tried to put aside my fears when I went over to Laurie's. The evening started promisingly enough. Laurie was cooking her favorite dish—fish in wine sauce and her special french fries. I was starved, having skipped lunch because it was right before the Math test. Stuie was at a friend's house. And Sylvia was in a good mood. She had had her hair cut and dyed. It was an embarrassing blonde. She's always mourned the loss of the "golden hair I used to have." Sylvia hasn't had golden hair since she was ten.

We made small talk and sat down to eat. The food was delicious.

"You really are a great cook," I complimented Laurie.

"I get it from my father," she grinned.

"Laurie!" Sylvia exclaimed in mock shock.

Silent munching.

"How were your exams?" Laurie garbled.

"Dear, don't talk with your mouth full," Sylvia said.

"Okay—except for Math."

"Ugh. Math. I'm sure mine was even worse."

"I always disliked Math," Sylvia smiled.

"So did I," Hank winked. He's a civil engineer. Sometimes I wonder if that's why my dad doesn't like to hang around with him very much.

"How were the rest of your exams?" I asked.

"Lousy."

"That's because you didn't study," I said lightly.

"Who said?"

"You weren't home last night."

Silence.

"Well, Laurie, I think it's time to tell Ruthie the big news."

"Big news?" I took a swallow of water. The french fry I was eating had suddenly stuck in my throat.

"It can wait, Mom," Laurie blushed.

"I think Laurie's right, Syl," Hank warned.

"Now is a fine time. We're all relaxed." Sylvia turned to me with a patronizing smile. "Ruthie, Mr. Simpson called."

"When?" I snapped, frightening even myself.

"Don't get so excited. Two days ago."

My head did a quick count. So, Laurie had lied to me that night. "Why didn't you tell me?" I was blurting things out.

"Mom, let me tell Ruthie," Laurie jumped in. "Look, I'm really sorry I didn't tell you the truth when you phoned, but Mr. Simpson said he wanted to see just me and Mom the next day. That's why I rushed off after my exam and didn't meet you."

"You saw him?"

"Yes, yesterday. Ruthie, I'm sorry. He said he doesn't want to handle a duo. 'Too hard to book,' he said."

"Sure. Look at Simon and Garfunkel. They even had to break up," I retorted. "So that's that, huh?"

No one said anything.

Finally Sylvia spoke, "Not quite, Ruth. Mr. Simpson is now Laurie's agent."

I stared uncomprehendingly first at her, then at Laurie. Laurie looked back helplessly.

"I told you this was not the time, Sylvia," Hank said.

"You're wrong, Hank. It's as good a time as any." My voice was hollow. "Betrayal knows no time."

"Ruthie, stop emoting," Sylvia jibed.

"Emoting? Look who's talking," my voice was shaking, rising.

"I tried to convince him," Laurie pleaded. "Didn't I, Mom?"

"Oh, I'll bet you did."

"She most certainly did, Ruth. Now face reality."

"What reality? What reality?" I had begun to shout.

"You are being unrealistic if you think Laurie should give up a career because of friendship."

"Friendship! Ha! She was never a friend."

Laurie started to cry. Hank left the room. I was so upset I didn't know what I was saying.

"How can you . . . ?" Sylvia began.

"Maybe she would've been a friend if it hadn't been for you." I flung out my arm, knocking over my water.

"Clean up that mess," Sylvia intoned coldly, thinking she was stopping the argument.

"You call that a mess?" I screamed. "I'll give you a mess." And I threw my plate on the floor.

Now, sitting here in my bedroom, I feel like an idiot, but then, it felt so good to throw something. I wished it had been Sylvia or Laurie. "I'm not your child. Clean it up yourself." And I ran out of the house.

It's not that I'm jealous. I just can't stand the lying, and the sneaking, and the trying to appease me with dinner. And I knew that Simpson was a creep. He's probably after Sylvia's ass. Wouldn't Mom love to hear me use that expression? I don't care. I feel mean.

Now that I think about it, I bet they invited me over because they want me to write Laurie's songs and help with her act. They can't just chuck me away—I've always been the more talented half of the team. So Laurie can sing and play the guitar. I'm the one who can sing and write the songs. I bet if I really tried I could learn to play the guitar too. Well, they can just beg me. I'm not writing one more song for Miss (she's no liberated woman) Laurie Stein. Let her *agent* find her a songwriter. She can find herself a new friend too. Who wants to be friends with a snake like her?

20

I got up early this morning and left a note saying not to worry. I had no direction in mind. I just decided to walk. June, and already it's boiling out. Even the half-hour trek to the coffee shop Laurie and I used to frequent seemed too long. When I got there, I was sweating, so I succumbed to the temptation of orange juice. I slid into the cracked seat of a booth. It was Saturday and there weren't many customers, so I figured Pruney Dyker wouldn't mind me sitting alone in the booth. No one knows Pruney Dyker's real name. He claims he was born wrinkled and got the nickname then. Every time anyone comes into his shop, he nods and drawls, " 'Lo." We all used to make up stories about Pruney coming from Texas and being a relic of the Old West—until we found out he's from New Jersey.

He hadn't seen me in months, but he still said, "'Lo," in exactly the same way. And when he came to take my order, he said, as always, "What'll it be?"

I was going to order my juice when I realized I'd never eaten breakfast alone in a coffee shop. And I was hungry. So, impulsively, I asked for juice, waffles, and tea. Mom still thinks I should drink milk every morning. Tea is reserved for dinnertime and when I'm sick. One morning, to be nice after the fight we'd had the night before, she served me a cup of tea. I demanded to know what was wrong and asked if she'd dropped cyanide in it. Needless to say, I blew my chances of having tea for breakfast again.

Just as I was starting on my waffles, Ms. Spielberg came in. I was so surprised, I nearly choked. Even though my booth was dark, she spotted me and came over.

"Hello. Mind if I join you?"

"No. But what are you doing here?"

"Oh, my husband and daughter are away and I didn't feel like cooking breakfast for myself. How about you?"

"It's my treat to myself."

"For finishing your exams?"

"Yes, I guess so," I muttered miserably.

Ms. Spielberg caught it. "What's up?"

"Nothing much—unfortunately. Laurie's got an agent who says duos are too hard to book."

"Ouch! Did she spring the news yesterday?"

"How did you know?"

"You've got on a morning-after face."

"Uh-oh. Sounds ugly."

"I wish I could improve on my advice, but all I can think of is what I told you before: be patient and stick with her."

"Stick with her! Do you know what she did? She lied to me, then invited me to dinner to soften the blow. I think that stinks." I was trembling and I felt tears well up.

Ms. Spielberg took my hand. "It does stink. But it also says that, clumsy as her methods were, she was trying to make you feel less bad about it."

"I don't believe it. I think she wanted to gloat."

"Did she gloat?"

I hesitated. Finally I had to admit she didn't. I began to cry into my waffles. Of course, Pruney picked just that moment to take Ms. Spielberg's order. She handed me a tissue. When I stopped, she said, "Did you tell her off?"

"Yes. Well, not *her* exactly. More her mother. I yelled a lot," I sniffled.

"Did that make you feel better?"

"No. Things came out nasty." I told her the story. When I got to the bit about Sylvia and Mr. Simpson, I felt really embarrassed, as though I were insinuating things that weren't actually happening. But Ms. Spielberg just listened quietly. When I had finished, she mused, "I think your friend is being taken for a ride—along with her mother. So do you."

"I do?"

"That's what you've suggested. Let's hope we're both wrong."

I wasn't really sure what she was referring to, but I tried to look as if I understood. I did feel that her words seemed gray, ominous.

"Laurie's certainly going to need you. In the meantime, you must have other good friends."

"Ha," I said cynically. Then I amended it, "Well, there's Lonnie. He's invited me to see his magic act tonight. Do you know him?"

"Uh-huh. He was one of my best students."

Suddenly, wanting to dispel the somber mood, I said jokingly, "How would you like to see his act? He told me I could bring friends."

She took me seriously, "Don't you think he'd be put off

by the appearance of a teacher, albeit a former one?"

"No, he's got a lot of self-confidence."

"Hmmm. Well, to tell you the truth, the thought of going to the movies on a Saturday night, which is what I'd planned, isn't very appealing. Sure, I'd love to come. Shall I pick you up?"

"You mean it? Wow!" And I excitedly gave her my address. I felt proud that my teacher was treating me like —well—a friend.

It wasn't until after she'd left that I began thinking I didn't much feel like bringing Ms. Spielberg and my parents together. I'd told each a lot about the other. I wanted to keep the circles separate. But then I thought she'd really enjoy meeting my grandma and vice versa. And I couldn't wait to see Lonnie's face. It's too bad Laurie wouldn't be part of the fun.

"What do you mean you just had breakfast out?" Mom demanded. "Do you think money grows on trees?" That's one of her favorite expressions.

"It was my allowance, Ma."

"That's not what your father gives you an allowance for."

"You give it to me."

"What?"

"You give it to me, not Dad."

"You'll worry him to death. Leaving a note! I caught him smoking a cigarette, he was so nervous. He's going to kill himself with his cigarettes," she yelled.

I decided to keep quiet.

She stopped and then spoke in a calmer voice, "What did you eat?"

"Huh? Oh, waffles."

"I never knew you liked waffles. Why haven't you ever asked me to make them?"

I shrugged.

"I bet you didn't have any milk. You know milk is good for you."

I knew it was time to change the subject. "Ma, I ran into Ms. Spielberg at Pruney's . . ."

"Pruney! How did that man get such a name?" she interrupted.

"Are you listening?"

"Yes, yes, go on. You met Ms. Spielberg at Pruney's."

"And I invited her to come with me to Lonnie's tonight."

"You never told me you were going to Lonnie's tonight."

"And she said 'yes.' "

"Why don't you ever tell me . . . She said 'yes'? Ms. Spielberg?"

"Yep. She's picking me up at seven thirty."

"She's coming here! Oh my God, look at this house. I have to vacuum and dust the living room. The carpet looks terrible. We don't have any cake. Where's Gram?"

I sighed. Off and running.

"Young lady, you get right to your room and clean it up."

"Ma, she's not going into my room."

"Clean it anyway . . . oh, Arthur." My dad had just entered. "Ruthie invited her teacher here tonight."

"She did?" Dad frowned.

"I didn't invite her here. She's just picking me up," I tried to get a word in. No such luck.

"And where were you this morning, Miss Big-Shot Zeiler?" Dad began.

"Mom'll tell you. I've got to clean my room," I said and shot upstairs. Even cleaning my room is better than listening to Dad bawl me out.

"Glad to meet you. Your daughter's a fine student," Ms. Spielberg firmly shook Dad's hand and spoke in her best teacher voice, only somewhat deflated by her blue jeans.

"Ruthie's always loved English. And she's raved about you," Mom chattered.

I winced. Ms. Spielberg smiled.

"Haf some cake. I baked it," Gram beamed.

"Just a bite," Ms. Spielberg twinkled.

"You Jewish?" Gram asked.

Mom looked embarrassed. She would've reserved that question for me. Dad disappeared into the living room.

"No. Greek. My husband's Jewish."

"You born there?"

"No, but my parents were. Where are you from?"

"Rumania. Greeks, Rumanians, Italians, Russians. We all peasants." Then, she laughed.

Ms. Spielberg laughed too. "Do you miss Rumania?"

"A little. I left young. Sometimes, I miss mountains and great, snowy winters."

"My mother misses hot summers."

"Oy, it plenty hot here for me," she sighed.

I giggled.

"What you leffing at? You don't know from snow. One day in Rumanian mountains and you'd cry, 'Gram, I can't go out. It too cold.'" She looked at me mischievously.

I fell for it. "That's what I say in New York."

"That's what I mean."

We all laughed.

"Well, we'd better get going," Ms. Spielberg said. She shook my parents' hands and then hugged Gram.

"Bet your mudder tell you to put on meat," Gram smiled.

"Momma," Mom squeaked in a pained voice.

"She does—and she's skinny as a rail."

"All children the same—and all mudders too."

We laughed again. Then, I gave her a hug too.

When we got into Ms. Spielberg's car, she said, "I love your grandmother."

"So do I." And I smiled.

Lonnie was surprised to see us. That's putting it mildly. He was shocked. He turned red and stumbled as he ushered us into the living room. No one was there.

"I thought you were putting on a performance," I said.

"I am," he mumbled.

"For just the two of us?"

"The others c-couldn't m-make it," he stuttered.

"Excuse me a moment," Ms. Spielberg went off to the bathroom.

Lonnie looked out the window.

"What gives?" I demanded.

"Aw gee, Ruthie," he turned to me, "I wanted to be alone with you."

"Alone with me? You told me to invite friends." Sometimes I'm really dense.

He frowned.

"Are you angry?" I asked. If I lost two friends in two days, I figured I might as well kill myself.

"No. Forget it." He still frowned.

Silence. I really didn't know what was happening.

Finally he said, "I'm leaving as soon as school ends. For the Cape."

"Oh. Well, it must be great up there."

"Yeah." He sat down next to me.

I looked at my hands. Ms. Spielberg was sure taking a long time.

Then, suddenly, he grabbed me awkwardly and kissed me. Really hard.

"Hey," I struggled, "Cut it out. You're hurting my arm."

His face was an even brighter red than before. "Haven't you been kissed before?" He scowled.

"Not like that," I lied. I'd never been kissed any which way—by a boy, that is. I thought I would've given anything to be kissed by Lonnie. But this wasn't the way I'd pictured it.

97

"I should've known better than to get mixed up with a sophomore," he jeered.

I was furious. I never expected that from Lonnie. I felt betrayed. First by Laurie, and now by Lonnie. Wheeling around, I spat out, "And I should have known I couldn't trust you. You're just like the other boys." I don't know what the other boys are like, but I can guess. Anyway, what I said stung him.

Just then, Ms. Spielberg returned. "On with the show," she said. Then she saw our faces. "Sorry, I appear to have interrupted something."

"No, you haven't," I said.

Lonnie stumbled to his feet. It was weird to see him so clumsy. He brought out the doves. We petted them and let them perch on our fingers. Then, Lonnie performed his tricks. He didn't goof up, but he also didn't have his usual flair.

"Bravo!" Ms. Spielberg applauded.

"Lonnie the Great," I cheered, somewhat sarcastically.

"Cokes?" he mumbled.

"Sounds good to me," Ms. Spielberg said, "Mind if I wander in your garden?" She disappeared outside.

Lonnie looked uncomfortable. Then, he turned to me. "I'm sorry," he said in a low voice, "I don't know what I was trying to prove."

I was feeling bold. Maybe because of all the letdowns. "Maybe you were doing what you heard guys are supposed to do."

"Maybe. But I'm not usually like that," he replied.

"Sure," I said, halfheartedly. I knew he was being honest, but I was still angry.

"I'm *really* not."

"Let's forget it."

We were silent.

Finally, he said, "Should I have asked you?"

"Asked me what?"

"If I could kiss you."

"I don't know. Maybe."

"May I kiss you now?"

"No."

He looked miserable. I felt sorry for him, but I really didn't want to be kissed. Not then. "Another time, maybe," I said.

He looked a little relieved. "I'll get the Cokes."

It was only after Ms. Spielberg dropped me off that I realized Lonnie really likes me. And I no longer had a best friend to tell that to.

21

I wonder what this great power is I have for getting rid of people. There's been no school this week so the teachers can mark exams and not only have I not seen Laurie, but I also haven't heard from Lonnie. Mort Schumsky had to leave on Saturday (he called while I was out), and had to cancel our beach date. Monday rained the entire day. I spent Tuesday hopefully looking up high-class camps in Cape Cod, knowing full well my parents can't afford them. Summer looks more and more bleak.

Twice this week I've watched Sylvia and Laurie, dressed fit-to-kill, drive off somewhere in the early afternoon. And the car's always back by the time I go home for dinner. I thought Laurie might've called me by now—at least to get permission to use my songs. I was thinking of calling her.

The plaque we won in the contest has been at her house for three weeks. We each agreed to keep it two weeks and then switch. Mom's been saying I'll never see the light of it. Anyway, I changed my mind about calling. Laurie might think I called to make up. No more going jellyfish for me.

I'm thinking of taking a modern dance class this summer. There's this teacher who's supposed to be very good. Some of her students have joined professional companies. Wouldn't Mom and Dad be surprised to have a dancer in the family? Ms. Spielberg thinks I should join a writers' workshop. She says my poems show a "unique sensibility." But you can't join the workshop here until you're sixteen.

I wonder what Laurie's doing.

22

I found out what Laurie's doing. A notice, printed cheaply,
my dad said later, came in the mail today. It read:

This Saturday Night
THE CAPRI CLUB
presents
THE SOFTONES, a mellow trio,
and
THE CHUCK CHARTERS COMBO
with Laurie Stafford, song-stylist
No cover.   No minimum.
The Capri Club
22 Lincoln Rd.
West Hempstead, New York

"Laurie Stafford" was circled and written next to it was, "That's Me! Laurie" in red ink.

I stared at it for a long time. Laurie Stafford, song-stylist. What the hell does that mean? And The Capri Club. Some dive I'd never heard of. What does that smart-ass think she's doing? And I thought Shelley Sugarman was bad! Laurie must have lied about her age. She always did look older. But how could she have gotten a job so soon? My head started to spin. She expected me to come see her too, little creep. Like hell I would—even if they'd let me in.

Then Mom came in and asked me what I was staring at. When she saw the notice she started to yell, "My God, who does she think she is? She'll be ruined by twenty. That Sylvia. No wonder everyone's beginning to talk."

"What are they saying?" I hadn't heard anyone talking.

"What? Oh nothing," she said hastily. "Just that Sylvia has no time for her kids anymore."

I wanted to yell that just because a person stays home doesn't mean she *has* time for her kids. Or understands them. I said nothing, but I felt rage building inside me.

"Well, you can find better friends," Mom went on. "Friends who act their age. By the way, what happened to that nice boy, Lonnie?"

"Nothing," I growled.

"What's the matter with you? You're not jealous of Laurie? You're much smarter than she is."

"I'm not jealous."

"Then what are you yelling for?"

"What's this?" Gram, her hands covered with soil, had just come in from the backyard.

"Just leave me alone," I screamed and ran out the door.

I went to my playground again and sat there, shaking. I hated Laurie. I hated Sylvia. I hated Lonnie. I hated Mom. I had no friends, no future.

When I calmed down, I realized somehow I had to go to The Capri Club on Saturday. If I didn't, everyone would say I was jealous, that I acted like a baby. But I couldn't figure out how to get in. Mom and Dad sure wouldn't take me. I wouldn't go with Hank and Sylvia. Oh hell!

At lunchtime, I dragged home. Mom and Gram had gone shopping and left me a sandwich in the fridge and a note which said: LONNIE CALLED. I had a flash and reached for the phone. I watched myself dial Lonnie's number and heard myself ask for him when his sister answered.

"Hello."

"Hi, Lonnie, it's Ruthie. You called?"

"Yeah."

Pause.

"I . . . uh . . . wanted to know what you were doing Saturday night?" He sounded strangely shy.

"I'm going to The Capri Club."

"Oh . . ."

"That is, if you'll take me."

"Huh? I never heard of it."

"Neither did I. But my friend Laurie's singing there."

"Oh. Okay."

"You will?"

"Sure. But wait a minute. Don't you have to be eighteen to get in?"

"Yeah, but you have a phony I.D., don't you?"

Another pause.

"No. I don't drink," he said in an embarrassed voice.

"Oh," I was terribly disappointed. Not that Lonnie doesn't drink, but now it seemed I'd never get in.

"Listen, what about your parents?" he asked.

"They don't drink either."

"No, I mean, couldn't they take us . . . er . . . you?"

"God! I'd never go with my parents."

"Oh."

Long pause. Then:

"I could ask my parents."

"You'd want to go out with your parents?"

"Well, it's my last weekend home," he gulped, "And I'd . . . um . . . like to see you. Friday I promised to . . ."

"Really?" I interrupted him, "Why? I mean, that's nice."

"Look, I'll ask them and call you back tonight."

I'm going to The Capri Club on Saturday night with Lonnie. I'm going to buy a new dress. When Laurie sees me, she'll turn green. So what if she's a singer? She's not going out with Lonnie Robbins. Mom is annoyed, but she won't say I can't go: Lonnie's Jewish and his father's a lawyer.

23

"I think it's lovely to double date with you and Lonnie,"
Ms. Robbins smiled as I got into their car.

I smiled back and guessed that "my date" was turning
red.

Ms. Robbins is a very vivacious, intelligent woman. She
teaches Sociology at a junior college in Queens and is a
firm believer in Culture, meaning that she goes to a lot of
plays and concerts and art films and clips articles out of
the *Times*. Actually, I like her—even if she does wear a wig
and makes silly remarks sometimes.

Mr. Robbins, on the other hand, likes to appear—well—
homespun or something like that. He's always talking
about Clarence Darrow. I read a play about him—*Inherit
the Wind* it was called—and I can see why Mr. Robbins

admires him. Unfortunately, Mr. Robbins is about as home-spun as a Cadillac, which is what he drives. Anyway, he's friendly and gentle—except I guess, in court.

"So, who is it we're going to hear? Your partner?" Mr. Robbins asked.

"Former partner," I said calmly.

"What happened to the team?"

"Went our separate ways. I'm more interested in dance anyway." I was trying that out to see how it felt.

"I didn't know you danced," Lonnie said, surprised.

"I don't—yet. I'm going to start lessons."

"I understand you write poetry," Ms. Robbins said. "Lonnie told me."

I think Lonnie could have cheerfully kicked his mother out of the car.

"Yes, I do."

"Keep it up. You might be another Emily Dickinson."

"Or Dorothy Parker." I smiled.

The Capri Club was perfect. Plastic paneling made to look like wood. Red vinyl seats. Red carpeting made of that washable stuff. Prints of Italian landscapes and jolly peasants. Very dark and very empty. A few people, probably "regulars," sat at the long, black bar.

We passed a young couple necking in a corner booth and a bored-looking couple at another on our way to a table near the stage. Then I saw Hank and Sylvia. They must've dumped Stuie with some poor baby-sitter because he wasn't there.

Sylvia saw me. "Ruthie, how nice!" she said loudly. Then she turned to the Robbinses. "How do you do. I'm Sylvia Stein. This is my husband, Hank."

"Hello," Mr. and Ms. Robbins looked puzzled.

"How's Laurie?" I asked.

"Oh, your daughter's performing," Ms. Robbins said.

"Yes. Laurie's just a bit nervous. . . . Excuse me," she looked toward the door. "I thought that was Mr. Simpson. We're expecting him."

"Sylvia, the man is not going to come. An agent doesn't come to performances," Hank sighed.

"I'm sure . . . ," Sylvia began.

"Hi, there. I'm Chuck Charters and we'd like to welcome you to The Capri Club."

"Enjoy the show," Sylvia whispered, and we stumbled to our table.

"I hope her agent is a good one," Mr. Robbins whispered confidentially. "You wouldn't believe how many shady characters pass themselves off as reputable agents."

"Shhhh, dear," Ms. Robbins said.

"We'd like to play a little number called 'Fly Me to the Moon,'" Chuck Charters announced.

They struck up the rottenest version of "Fly Me to the Moon" I've ever heard. Lonnie and I looked at each other and giggled.

"Let's dance," he said mischievously.

"You kidding?"

"No. Come on."

So we danced around the floor, laughing and stepping on each other's feet. When we finished, Mr. and Ms. Robbins applauded us.

"Thank you," Chuck Charters said, looking in our direction, "Next, 'The Shadow of Your Smile.'"

"Ugh! Excuse me," Lonnie said. "Hey, Dad, order me a drink, will you?"

"Gin and tonic?" Mr. Robbins wisecracked.

"Very funny. A Coke."

"My son the alcoholic," Mr. Robbins grinned as Lonnie went off to the men's room.

"Isn't my son delicious?" Ms. Robbins whispered to me.

I coughed violently.

"Drink for you?" Mr. Robbins asked, patting me on the back.

"Ginger ale," I choked. Wouldn't Lonnie love knowing his mother found him delicious!

The Softones were as bad as Chuck Charters, only they sang "Fly Me to the Moon," or something like it in three-part harmony. Finally, after three more songs I would rather not have heard, "Laurie Stafford" came out, loudly applauded by her parents. She was wearing a long, silver gown and a white boa around her neck. This time I choked for real and grabbed for my ginger ale.

"Holy cow!" Lonnie gasped.

"How old is she?" Ms. Robbins asked.

"Fourteen," I said.

"That doesn't look like the girl who sang with you," Mr. Robbins said.

"It's not," I snorted.

"I thought . . . ," Mr. Robbins began.

"That's a joke, Walter," Ms. Robbins said.

"I'd like to sing," Laurie sounded funny, sort of like she was putting on an English accent, "a wonderful old song called 'I'm in the Mood for Love.'"

What is this? my mind yelled. Who's she trying to be? She sang in a hokey style, as Chuck Charters assaulted the piano. Who the hell was her voice teacher?

Lonnie and I looked at each other.

"Thank you, thank you," she bowed, "Now a song Ethel Merman made famous—'I've Got Rhythm.'"

Ethel Merman! What was happening to her? I always thought she had a good voice, but her pretty soprano wasn't at all suited to Ethel Merman songs. And anyway, this isn't the 1930s.

Soon, she went into a medley of Rodgers and Hammerstein numbers, climaxing with "The Sound of Music." When she finished, Ms. Robbins said, "Dear me, I mean, very nice."

"Don't be polite for my sake," I said miserably, "It was awful. I don't know what they've done to her."

"She needs a better agent," practical Mr. Robbins said.

"For my final number, I'd like to sing a song a very dear friend of mine wrote. I understand she's in the audience. Ruth Zeiler, stand up. Give her a hand."

Who did she think she was? Ed Sullivan? I stayed in my seat.

"It's called 'Right Now.' "

"Oh no," I gritted my teeth.

"What is it?" Ms. Robbins said.

"It's the song she and Laurie sang at the contest," Lonnie explained.

"Oh no," I moaned.

He reached for my hand.

When Laurie had finished, I said, "I'm sorry, I don't feel too well. May we leave?"

"Certainly," Mr. Robbins said.

"Don't you want to congratulate your friend?" Ms. Robbins asked.

"I'll call her tomorrow," I said feebly.

Silently, I thought, bet you don't know *what* I'll call her.

Lonnie walked me to my door. "Sorry about Laurie," he said.

"Yeah."

"I think I understand."

"Yeah."

"Um . . . can I kiss you good night?"

"Why not?" I sure wasn't very encouraging.

He kissed my cheek.

110

"You don't have to be *that* cautious," I said.

He kissed my mouth. "Good night."

"Night."

"So how was it?" Mom asked as soon as I got in.

"Not bad," I lied.

"That's all you have to say?"

"I'll tell you about it tomorrow. I'm tired."

"Ten o'clock and you're tired? That doesn't sound like you."

"Well, it's me, all right." I shrugged and went to my room.

24

I spent the morning looking at ads for cheaper Cape Cod camps and having a large debate with myself about calling Laurie. At four in the afternoon, I finally decided it would be the grown-up thing to do. Hank answered the phone.

"Ruthie. I'm glad you called. Sylvia and Laurie are at The Capri Club."

"Now?"

"For a photography session."

"Oh."

"Ruthie, do you think you could come over? I'd like to talk with you."

"Uh." I didn't feel like hearing another lecture.

"It's important." He sounded sort of desperate. I was surprised. Hank is always so calm.

"Okay," I agreed.

"Who was that?" Mom asked, when I got off the phone, "Your good friend, Laurie?"

"No, it wasn't, and do you have to rub it in?" I snapped.

"I just want you to realize you don't need her."

"I'm going out."

"Where?"

"California."

"Don't get smart."

"Okay." And I dashed out.

"It's Toothie Ruthie," Stuie grunted.

"It's P-Uey Stuie," I responded.

"Aw, your mother," he sneered.

I wonder who he's been hanging around with.

"Stuie, get lost," Hank called. "Come in, Ruthie."

I walked into the kitchen. I felt funny. First, because I hadn't been there for a while. Second, because I never went over just to see Hank.

"Iced tea?" he asked.

"Sure." I love iced tea even more than hot tea.

"Report cards tomorrow, eh?"

"Yep."

"Laurie's worried."

"Me too—about Math."

"How are your parents?" he said, after a pause.

"Okay."

He was obviously fishing for things to say.

"Who was the good-looking fellow you were with last night?"

"Lonnie Robbins."

"The magician?"

"Yeah."

"His father's a lawyer?"

"Uh-huh."

"Good."

Another pause. I wondered what he meant by "good." Good for Mr. Robbins? For Lonnie? For me?

"What did you think of the show?"

I knew he was eventually going to ask me that, but the question jarred me anyway. "It was okay," I answered weakly.

"It stank. You don't have to spare my feelings."

"It wasn't *that* bad. But I don't understand Laurie's act."

"You and I both. Sylvia said something about Simpson's feeling that a girl who can sing 'classic pop tunes' could be the up and coming thing. It's unique, he claims."

"But Laurie's voice is all wrong for that stuff. And that outfit made her look like a kid trying to pretend she's a grown-up." I stopped. I thought I had said too much.

"Absolutely right, but tell that to Sylvia." He smiled ruefully.

"Still, if that's what Simp . . . er . . . Mr. Simpson thinks is best."

"Ruthie, I've been doing some investigating of Mr. Simpson. You see, we've been spending quite a bit of money—several photography sessions, interviews. . . ."

"Interviews!" I exclaimed. I tried to imagine Laurie telling the story of her meteoric rise to fame. "I owe it all to my mom" and stuff like that.

"Sheet music, lessons, costumes, plus agent's fees," Hank continued. "Simpson's had to travel a lot and make contacts. You know, taking people out to lunch and all. I didn't realize that Sylvia had paid him an advance until I got the cancelled checks." He stopped abruptly. I felt weird listening to that stuff. It didn't seem any of my business.

"Well, he did get Laurie a job already," I said.

"Yes, a job," he said slowly, "But last night I overheard something I'm going to look into. I think Simpson owns a sizable interest in The Capri Club."

114

I looked at him blankly. I couldn't figure out why he was telling me all this. "Is that illegal?" I asked, trying to sound intelligent.

"I don't think it's actually illegal. But it isn't exactly on the up and up. It means Simpson is not only getting his 10 percent, but profits from the club."

"Hmm," I hummed wisely.

"I think he books his clients into that club so he can get money from all ends."

"Then, is Simpson a 'shady character'?" I asked, remembering Mr. Robbins' words.

"That's what I'm afraid of, Ruthie."

What he was saying dawned on me slowly. "You think Laurie and Sylvia are being taken for a ride," I said, remembering Ms. Spielberg's words.

He nodded sadly.

"But why are you telling me this?" I finally said.

He clinked the ice in his glass. "You're Laurie's best friend."

Was, I thought.

"I think she's going to need you."

I sighed. The same tune.

"I just want you to . . . be around," Hank said quietly.

"I'm planning on going to camp," I protested.

"But you won't be leaving right away, will you?"

"I guess not," I frowned.

"You're a good girl, Ruthie," Hank said.

I got embarrassed. "I've got to go now, Hank."

"Okay. Thank you for coming over."

"Thank you for the iced tea," I said quickly and left.

All night I pondered over what Hank told me. I didn't quite understand it, but it sounded nasty. I decided to ask Mr. Robbins about "shady characters." Maybe he could help the Steins.

As for being Laurie's friend, well, she'll have to call me.

25

"I'm leaving next week for the Cape," Shelley gushed to Roz.

We were sitting in homeroom, waiting for our report cards. It's so dumb—we have to sit there for an hour just so the school gets money, or something like that. I was trying not to bite my nails. Last year I used to sit in class and clean my nails with a compass point. I stopped when I noticed that Shelley and Roz were looking at me and giggling.

"I wish I were going away," Roz sighed.

"What are you doing, Ruthie?" Shelley called, "Visiting Lonnie at the Cape?"

"I might," I said smoothly, "I'm going to camp there—probably."

116

"Oh, you'll love it. And then you can see me perform!"
Shelley exclaimed.

"Do they let you leave camp?" Roz asked.

"Of course," I answered, but I wasn't sure.

"All right, class, here they are," Mr. Elroy announced,
holding up a stack of report cards. "When I call your name,
get your card and leave. Immediately."

It's times like that I hate having a last name that begins
with "Z."

"Robert Andrews," Mr. Elroy called.

I looked out the window.

"Ronald Andrews." As usual, he was absent.

"Susan Bellink."

Susan looked at her card and began to cry.

"Mary Bellinky."

On and on went the roll. I had started to nibble my
nails. The room had gotten very still except for the squeal
or cry or giggle or shout from the person who had just
received his or her card.

"Roz Schecter."

Roz took her card, peeked at it and yelled, "I passed!"

"Louis Schneider."

Poor Louis had flunked French since seventh grade.

"Flunked again," he shouted and waved. The rest of us
cheered.

"Shelley Sugarman."

Shelley confidently opened her card. "Cape Cod, here
I come," she said and flew out.

"Lindsay Taylor."

More Ts.

I tried to read the book I had brought.

Finally, "Well, Ruth, you're the last one."

I took my card. Mr. Elroy was smiling at me. I waited
to open it until he started fumbling with his papers.

I got 95 in English, 80 in History, 85 in Biology, 90 in French, 70 in Phys. Ed., and I passed Math. Cape Cod, here I come.

Outside school, I met Lonnie. Funny, I didn't see Laurie at all.

"You pass?" he smiled.

"Yep. Even Math."

"Me too."

"Great!"

"I'm leaving tomorrow."

"Yeah."

"Can I see you tonight?"

"I think so," I smiled.

"Great. Eight o'clock?"

"Sure."

I just have to get to Cape Cod!

26

"I knew you'd pass," Mom said, "But couldn't you do better than 65?"

"Mom," I sighed.

"For that, I make you special meal," Gram grinned, "Toikey." Then, she laughed. "Just making joke. I bake choclat cake."

"Yum!" I yelled and rushed for the kitchen.

"Well, your father'll be glad you passed. Maybe he'll take us out to dinner."

"Not tonight, Mom, I'm seeing Lonnie."

"Why can't we ever do anything together anymore?" she whined.

"Ma, he's leaving tomorrow."

"Oh." And she shut up.

After dinner, the phone rang.

"I bet Lonnie can't make it," Mom said and went to the phone. That's what I love best about her—her optimism!

"You'll try to do better next year?" Dad asked.

"Yes," I sighed.

"Ruthie, it's Laurie," Mom said in her surprise-surprise voice.

"Laurie?" I asked.

"Laurie. You know, your good *friend*."

I sauntered to the phone. "Hello," I said coolly.

"Hi, Ruthie. It's me. I wanted to know how you did." She sounded strained.

"Did what?"

"On your report card."

"Oh. I passed everything. You?"

"I flunked M-math," her voice cracked, "and Earth Science." She started to cry.

"Gee, I'm sorry." Served her right, I thought.

"C-could you c-come over?" she wailed.

The foul-weather friend! "I'm afraid I'm busy . . ."

"S-something else happened, too," she moaned.

"What?" I did have my suspicions, though.

"Please come over."

I paused. She sounded really troubled. But tonight was going to be my last night with Lonnie for months.

"Please," she begged.

I finally gave in. "Okay, but just for a little while." I figured I could call Lonnie and tell him to make it later.

Hank answered the door. "Glad you came, Ruthie," he said, "She's downstairs."

I went into the playroom. Laurie was sitting on the sofa, looking awful. Her eyes were red, her nose was running, and her hair looked like someone had sat on it. I sat down next to her.

"Hi, kid," I said.

"Wahhh," she howled and flung herself in my arms.

I patted her back and handed her a tissue. "Okay, tell Ruthie," I said when she stopped bawling.

"It w-was all a f-fake," she sniffled.

"What was?"

"Mr. S-Simpson. He's a c-crook."

"He is?" I feigned surprise.

"He's skipped town."

"Skipped town?"

"With a lot of our m-money," and she started to cry all over again.

This time I was surprised. It took awhile to get out the story and even then it was all confused. Anyway, it seems yesterday Mr. S. took a large advance from Sylvia to produce a "property" that seemed "just right" for Laurie. Some musical, apparently. When Sylvia told Hank about it, he turned pale and asked if it was cash or a check she'd given him. It turned out to be cash, unfortunately. Hank had just gotten word about Simpson's share in The Capri Club. Today, they called at his office and discovered it was for rent. Poor Mort Schumsky. I bet he doesn't know his brother's a crook.

"It's not even so much the money," Laurie said, "It's just so . . . so . . . humiliating!"

"Well, at least you'll know better next time," I said.

"Next time! Forget it. No more performing for me. I'm going to be a nurse."

I stifled a giggle.

We sat quietly for a while. Then Laurie asked, "How are you?"

"Not bad."

"Lonnie is cute. Is it serious?"

"Very," I said sarcastically, "Which reminds me, can I use your phone?"

Lonnie was really disappointed and so was I, but sometimes, you have to do something even if it isn't the thing you'd most like to do. And anyway, a best friend is a best friend.

When I returned, Laurie turned to me shyly, "I guess I've been pretty creepy. I'm sorry."

"Okay," I said.

"Ruthie. I missed you."

"Humph," I humphed.

"Want to continue The Dream?"

"No, let's talk," I said.

"About what?"

"I think we've got plenty to talk about."

When I left, Hank whispered, "Thanks a lot, Ruthie."

"For what?" I whispered back.

"For being around."

"Oh. How's Sylvia?"

"Not too well right now. She's got a migraine. She'll get over it, though."

"Yeah. Well, good night."

I can't believe school's ended. Next year I'll be a junior. And Lonnie'll be a senior. Maybe I'll get to go to the Senior Prom. Ha-ha! But now I've got a whole summer ahead of me. I guess I'll be staying around here after all —except for my trip to Cape Cod. It's not so bad. And it's cheap. And I guess I'll get a lot of writing done. I think my style is maturing.